# THE GUARDIAN
## Clan Ross of Skye

**The Guardian: Clan Ross of Skye**
*USA Today Bestselling* **Author**
**Hildie McQueen**

Copyright © 2025 by Hildie McQueen
Print Edition

All rights reserved. No part of this book may be reproduced in any form or by any electronic or mechanical means—except in the case of brief quotations embodied in critical articles or reviews—without written permission.

The characters and events portrayed in this book are fictitious. Any similarity to real persons, living or dead, is purely coincidental and not intended by the author.

**He broke her heart once. She'll be damned if she lets it happen again.**

Ailith Shaw once gave her heart to Hendry McNichol—only to watch him walk away shattering her heart. Now widowed, impoverished, and fiercely independent, she scrapes by in the shadow of the very clan she blames for her husband's death. The last thing she needs is a guard from that cursed clan forcing his protection on her… especially if it's *him*.

**She doesn't need a champion. But he's never stopped wanting to be hers.**

Once a reckless warrior, Hendry McNichol is now a loyal guard to the laird—and a man haunted by the choices that cost him the woman he loved. He let Ailith slip through his fingers once, and she married his rival. Now, he'll risk everything to shield her from the brewing tensions, even if she despises him and refuses to admit the fire between them still burns.

# CHAPTER ONE

*Autumn, Ross Keep, Isle of Skye*

"Are ye certain ye need to return to the keep so soon?" Hendry McNichol's mother asked, her hands cupping his face. "Ye arrived just the day before yesterday."

Every time he visited it was the same; his mother's reluctance to bid him farewell reminded him how blessed he was to have such loving parents.

His father came up behind her and gave him a warm smile. "Be with care, son, and come back within a fortnight. I will roast a lamb, and we will invite the fair Meredith and her family for supper."

Hendry wanted to groan. Another reason he cut most visits short was because of his parents' quest to get him married off. It didn't matter that his brother, Ethan, and sister, Arlene, both had a gaggle of children. To his parents their children were not fully grown until they were married and producing offspring.

"I will do my best," he promised, bending to kiss his mother's cheeks and then his father's. "I'd best go. My duties begin first thing in the morning."

It was another long period before he was finally mounted and heading from his father's small farm on the outskirts of Ross lands to Ross keep. He'd grown up playing in the forest around the farm, rarely seeing people other than the farmers' families who lived nearby. There was little need for anything that required a trip to the village or to seek the laird's help. His father and their neighbors lived a peaceful existence with very little discord.

It wasn't until Hendry was ten and five that he had his first encounter with the laird's guards. Mounted on huge horses, the equally impressive warriors had stopped at each farm to inform them of a threat by the Mackinnon's, a rival clan.

He'd been awestruck; so much so, he and his brother had raced after the men and trailed them to the next farm just to watch how they carried themselves with assurance and an air of fearlessness.

After that day, he'd been obsessed with the idea of one day becoming like those brave men.

Guiding his stead along the familiar road toward the keep, Hendry kept a watchful eye, something ingrained after years at the service of the laird. It was when a man's guard was down that danger struck.

A hare darted into the road, stopped, and stared at his horse for a split second before dashing back into the safety of the forest. He couldn't help but chuckle at the small creature giving into curiosity before fleeing.

Just as he turned his attention back to the road, movement between the trees got his attention. Hendry pulled the horse to a stop and watched as three men with bows and quivers strapped to their backs traveled on foot.

One held a strap with two rabbits. The other two held various small creatures they'd killed.

For a moment, he considered stopping them and ensuring

they'd received permission from Laird Ross to hunt, but seeing they'd only killed enough to feed their families, he decided to let it pass.

He continued on, looking forward to the familiarity of what he felt was home. Although returning to his family's dwelling was always fulfilling, it was not where he lived. The keep, his quarters there, was truly his home.

A usual stop on the route was a small creek where he stopped to water his horse and if needed, himself as well. The clear water gurgled as it passed through the rock bed, the soothing sound beckoning the thirsty to come.

His horse went to the edge and drank greedily. They'd not traveled far, but like him, the steed was always sure to drink and eat plenty. One never knew when the next meal or water source would come when in battle or traveling.

"We will be home shortly," he told the animal. "No need to act as if in a drought."

Hendry went to one knee and cupped his hands, dipped them in the water, and lifted the refreshing liquid to his lips. He repeated it twice before stopping and looking around.

A warrior was always aware of his surroundings, of the changes in noise. The ceasing of birds' calls, and the shifts in the air. The first thing that caught Hendry's attention was a group of birds taking flight, as if startled.

Straining to listen, the unmistakable crunch of leaves meant movement. There was a soft noise, perhaps a whisper by someone thinking themselves covert. Whether human or beast, to Hendry it was clear he was not alone.

It was better to be safe than not, Hendry pulled his sword from the scabbard across his back and pretended to study it, as if assessing its need to be cleaned or sharpened at the creek's edge. The entire time he strained, listening to ensure all was well before mounting.

A rock flew through the air, striking his mount. The startled animal cried out, moving away from Hendry, just as two men rushed from the woods' edge toward him.

Keeping their distance, they stopped in front of him. One slightly to the right, the other to the left.

"Hand over yer money pouch," a bearded man with matted hair ordered, pointing his dagger at him. "I never miss my target," he said, winding the dagger between his fingers.

"Throw it here," the other bedraggled man called out. A short sword in his hand. "We won't wait long."

Hendry stuck his hand into the belt of his pants, pretending to untie his pouch whilst taking a pair of steps toward the man who held the sword. Although he didn't doubt he'd be able to dispatch this one, he had to remain wary of the one with the dagger.

The man with the sword took steps backward and glared at him. "Do I as we say, or we will kill ye."

"This is nae yer first time robbing someone. Is it?" Hendry asked, stopping all pretense of untying the pouch. He held his sword toward the man nearest and took quick steps to close the distance.

The man with the sword began swinging wildly, his wide eyes moving to the one who held a dagger, as if asking why it took so long for him to throw.

Ensuring to keep moving, Hendry did his best to avoid being struck by a dagger while blocking against the wide swings. If not for the danger of death, he would find parrying against such an untrained fighter hilarious.

"If ye dinnae stop, ye will hurt yerself," he teased, as he swung his sword with a swift motion cutting across the man's wrist sending the man's sword flying.

The man grabbed his injured hand, and while yelling out curses, he ran to stand behind the other man, who now held a dagger in each hand.

Instinct told Hendry that this one was lethal. It was in the eyes. Men who killed and enjoyed it, had hollow empty eyes. All humanity had been replaced with a need to kill again. The intoxicating exhilaration of domination, and the thrill of taking a life becomes nigh irresistible to men like that.

Keeping his attention on the man's hands, he moved across toward his steed, hoping to grab his shield. The first dagger flew across the air. Hendry saw it, jerked sideways, but the weapon managed to cut through his left side.

The grungy man cackled. "I can kill ye where ye stand and take yer coin. Be a good boy and save me the trouble."

Hendry wasn't fooled. The man was enjoying the hunt, wanted to prolong the time between injuring him and killing him.

"I am a guard for Laird Ross. Be on yer way," Hendry growled. "Ye will nae win."

Again the man cackled, this time joined by the other one. "I beg to differ," the man replied.

Hendry watched the man's hand, concentrating so as to see when he flicked his wrist in hopes of avoiding the dagger.

Just as the man lifted his hand, his eyes moved past him. Unsure if it was a trick to take his attention away, Hendry refused to look.

At first, he wasn't sure what had happened. The sharp pain on his right side was startling. A second later, he realized it had not been a trick. Another person had come from behind and plunged a blade into him. A blow to the back of the head made a sick cracking sound, and Hendry fell face-first into the dirt. His vision swam as he struggled to get to all fours. It proved impossible, and he collapsed just as darkness took over.

SOMETHING NUDGED HIM. Hendry fought to open his eyes until finally he could see light. Everything swayed, as if the world was tilting until he had to close his eyes to keep from throwing up. Waves of nausea and an excruciating headache made it hard for him to get up.

Another nudge and he turned his head to the right and peeked through barely open eyes. It was his horse. The creature appeared to be aware something was amiss with Hendry.

"I am alive horse," he grunted. "Stop moving me."

The horse responded by shoving his large nose against Hendry's face, seemingly glad to hear him speak.

It took a while before he finally pushed from the ground onto his knees. His stomach rolled, and he crawled on all fours to the creek. Each movement sending shards of pain down his sides where he'd been cut. The injuries, headache, and nausea made for a miserable trek.

At last, Hendry reached the stream. He staggered to his knees and plunged his face into the water, the cold bite shocking his skin. He drank deeply. The chill easing the fire in his throat, but the true torment throbbed inside his skull.

He threw up, dry heaving once his stomach was empty.

Each time, his left side protesting with piercing pain.

It took colossal effort to climb onto the horse. The injury on his right side was not deep, but stab had fully penetrated through his side, but it had cut deeply enough that blood seeped through his tunic. The blow to the head was causing the disorientation and a headache so piercing, he wanted to pull his hair out.

The nearest place he could go was the cottage belonging to Ailith Shaw. A widow who never ceased to hide her disdain for him. Unfortunately, he had to get shelter somewhere. Staying in the woods could prove fatal if the bandits returned to ensure he was truly dead or if he bled out.

Hendry's head swam, his vision blurring and clearing. Every glint of sunlight that filtered through the trees made him flinch, the brightness like shards of glass to his sensitive eyes. The headache persisted, and several times his stomach tumbled, but as nothing was left in his stomach, the nausea made him lean to the side and dry heave. Hendry clung to consciousness by sheer will, his grip slack on the reins, his body swaying like a drunkard in the saddle. Each step the horse took jarred his wound. He muttered curses under his breath.

Just when he was on the verge of giving up and finding a place to hide in some foliage, Ailith's humble cottage came into view.

He didn't dismount. He collapsed. His boots hit the ground first, knees buckling as he dropped out of the saddle and stumbled toward the door. His body gave a final protest, swaying violently before he slumped down beside the threshold. With trembling fingers, he reached out and knocked...three weak raps.

A dog barked from within, a furious warning. Then silence.

No footsteps. No voice. No sign of her.

He lifted his hand again to knock but froze as a surge of nausea rose like a wave and crashed over him. He fell forward onto all fours, heaving again. Pain tore through his side, the wound feeling as if tearing open, fresh blood dripped soaking into the dirt. But the aching was nothing compared to the dagger cleaving through his skull.

With sweat slicking his brow, blood darkening his tunic, and the world spinning beneath him, Hendry slumped against the doorframe and closed his eyes. If he was to die, at least she would inform the laird, who would, in turn, send a messenger to his family.

With a shaking hand, he drew letters into the dirt.

*Three men two bearded.*

Once again blessed blackness closed in, lifting away the pain and granting him rest.

# CHAPTER TWO

Alith rarely ventured into the woods without Teller, her fiercely loyal companion, but that morning the dog had limped across the garden whining with every step. She'd checked his paw for thorns or cuts but found nothing. She figured that perhaps he'd twisted it or something and needed to rest it. Still, she hated leaving him behind.

Teller had whined low when she slipped out with her basket, his protest pitiful enough to make her pause at the edge of the trees. But necessity pushed her forward. She needed the herbs desperately. Her coin purse was nearly empty, and without dried bundles and salves to sell at market, there'd be no money for flour. Let alone for the inexpensive fabric she'd been eyeing so she could make herself something to wear as most of her clothing was threadbare.

The forest was quiet, eerily so. No birdsong. Only the crunch of her boots over dry leaves and the rustle of her skirt as she moved quickly through the underbrush. She'd just plucked a cluster of yarrow when deep, male voices broke through the stillness.

She froze, her breath catching.

Dropping low, she shoved her basket into a thick patch of leaves and crawled behind a thorny bramble. The thud of hooves echoed closer: heavy and purposeful. Not a casual ride.

Not the easy pace of merchants or the laird's guards on routine patrol. These riders sounded determined.

Ailith pressed herself into the earth, barely breathing. The path, a crooked ribbon through the woods, was only yards away. If one of them so much as turned their head, they'd see her.

She didn't trust strangers. Not out here. Alone, unarmed, and without Teller. She was too easy a target. She'd heard many stories of women pulled from paths, dragged into trees, found barely alive or never seen again at all.

Her pulse roared in her ears. All she could do now was stay hidden… and pray they passed her by.

The closer they came, the drier Ailith's throat became. As if fear itself had stolen every drop of moisture from her body. Her heart pounded a furious rhythm in her chest. Her body was tense and still, every instinct screaming to stay hidden.

Then she saw them.

Through a narrow slit in the foliage, she caught glimpses of three men emerging from the shadows of the trees. They looked as if just been in a fight. Cloaks torn. Faces streaked with grime. Eyes wild.

"He was gone," one of them grumbled.

"By now the bastard's dead," another said with a laugh that cracked through the forest too loudly for the quiet surroundings.

Another laughed, low and without mirth, as he slapped his companion on the back. "Aye, he probably crawled somewhere and died. We've enough coin now for drink and a warm wench or two."

The first one who'd spoken pointed toward the village. "To

the pub!" he bellowed, voice sharp with triumph.

Ailith's eyes locked onto the crimson stain that darkened the man's sleeve there was no mistaking what it was. Blood.

She bit back a gasp, clutching the ground beneath her as if it could swallow her whole. Murderers. They'd killed someone and were now heading toward Tokavaig as if returning from a victorious hunt.

The stink of blood and sweat clung to the air as they passed. Fortunately, they'd not once glanced her way.

Only when their laughter had faded into the trees did Ailith allow herself a full breath.

AILITH WAITED UNTIL long after the men disappeared from view before grabbing her basket and scurrying back into the trees. But she couldn't seem to slow her heart, her mind, or her feet. She found she could not relax even surrounded by the forest. It wasn't a short walk to reach her cottage, and she longed for the promise of refuge from danger it provided.

Somehow she had to figure out a way to get word to the laird or the village constable about what she'd seen. Though not today. Today, it was best to remain safe at home. Tomorrow, she'd be able to think more clearly.

As she approached the back of her house, Ailith was able to take a long breath and release the tension. It was a humble home, made of stone and wood. But it was also well-built and sturdy, providing her safety from danger.

Teller was barking even before she opened the door. The dog rushed out as soon as she pulled it open and raced around the cottage, not even bothering with a greeting.

It was strange, but perhaps the dog was in a hurry to relieve himself. Ailith went inside and pulled the door firmly closed. Teller would scratch at the door to be let back inside.

Despite the interruption of the men, she'd managed to almost fill her basket. But before she got busy hanging the herbs to dry, she decided to have some cider and warm up the leftover stew. Her fright and hurried return home had left her more than a bit hungry.

There was noise at the front door from Teller, more of a whine than a bark. It was the noise he often made when he'd caught a squirrel or a rabbit.

"Good dog," Ailith called out, hopeful that it was a large hare, which she would prepare for supper.

Upon throwing the door open, Teller was not in the opening. She quickly looked to the right, nothing. To the left… all the air left her lungs.

There was a man slumped over, and Teller was licking his face.

It had to be the man. The dead man. The one those men most assuredly had killed. Her mind swam as she scanned the area trying to figure out what she should do next. Noting a horse grazing not far off, she immediately recognized the beautiful golden-brown steed. It belonged to Hendry.

Her heart caught in her throat, and for a long moment she was frozen to the spot. Then slowly, she stepped out of her cottage and lowered to look at him.

He was very still, eyes closed, head lolled to the side. Hendry's face was covered in sweat and dirt, but still she couldn't help but notice how handsome he was. Examining him for injuries, she noted that blood seeped from his side forming a dark pool on the ground.

With shaky fingers, she reached to touch his exposed neck and was relieved when a steady pulse vibrated where she touched.

"Hendry," she gently patted his cheek. "Can ye hear me?"

His eyelids fluttered, but there was no other response.

"Hendry, ye must wake. I cannae possibly bring ye inside on my own."

Again, there was no response. Ailith looked to Teller. "I suppose we will have to find a way. And ye will help me."

After rushing inside and grabbing one of her threadbare blankets, she came back out and spread it on the ground next to Hendry. Then as carefully as she could, she pushed and pulled him until he lay, for the most part, atop it.

"Come, Teller," she called to the dog. "Pull."

Thankfully, she'd taught him the command since a pup, pulling with rags, teaching him to tug. It had come in handy many times when she'd required help dragging bundles of wood and such back to their home.

The dog obediently bit into the end of the blanket she'd held out to him and together, little by little, they were able to drag the unconscious man into the cottage.

By the time Hendry lay just past the entry where she could close the door, both she and the dog were panting from the arduous task of dragging the heavily muscular warrior inside.

SHE MADE SEVERAL trips to the well, filling two buckets with water then her pot and setting it over a newly started fire to boil. Ailith pushed hair back from her face as she began the work of cutting away his tunic.

To her surprise, the injury wasn't as bad as she'd expected.

It was a clean cut and should have missed anything vital. She'd practiced healing long enough to know what was and wasn't life-threatening, and this stab wasn't. However having lost so much blood was concerning.

After cleaning the wound, she packed it with a poultice and clean bandages, then wrapped his midsection.

If she didn't find the reason for his loss of consciousness, he could perish. Her heart thundered with dread.

Despite it being an examination to possibly save his life, Ailith couldn't help feeling awkward when running her hands down his chest, then his sides. Finally, she turned him onto his side and did the same to his back until she came to the belted britches he wore. She found a shallow cut on his right side, but it wasn't bleeding.

"It cannae be helped," she said out loud as she pushed down the clothing from his hips.

There were no visible injuries that she could see. Ailith took a deep breath as she lowered him carefully onto his back.

Her eyes went directly where they shouldn't… Gulping at the intrusion, she quickly looked away.

There had been a time when she'd had his body pressed against her. When they'd spent stolen moments together, exploring one another, touching each other's bodies until there was a familiarity between them. Hendry had been her first love. The man she'd been sure she'd spend the rest of her life with.

It was not meant to be, and yes, as she studied his handsome face and powerful body, she couldn't help the thoughts, as she often had, of what could've been.

The fire in the hearth crackled bringing her out of her musings.

Ailith quickly finished removing his blood-soaked britches and boots, leaving him bare as the day he was born, and began inspecting each muscular leg. Once again, she'd not found any injury.

Working with care, her cloth glided swiftly from his neck to his ankles, wiping away sweat and dirt with gentle strokes. Every pass of the damp linen gave her another chance to search for other wounds, yet again she found nothing. No gashes. No bruises. Just the lean, powerful form of a man who had been perfectly created.

Then her gaze snapped to his head.

*Foolish girl,* she cursed inwardly. She hadn't checked for a blow to his head. Heart hammering, Ailith ran her fingers through the thick waves. Her fingertips searched his scalp, parting strands with care until she reached the base of his skull near the nape.

Her breath caught.

A swollen lump rose beneath her touch. Dried blood clung to the matted strands, and when she withdrew her hand, her fingers were streaked crimson. She let out a breath she'd been holding.

Thank God his hair had staunched the bleeding, but that changed little. Head wounds were treacherous. Slow to show their toll and often times fatal.

He needed to wake.

She rushed to her small bedchamber, snatched two thick blankets, and rolled them tightly around logs from the hearth. Returning to his side, she lifted his head gently and slid the makeshift props beneath his neck and shoulders, elevating him to ease the pressure.

Once he was settled, she pulled a fresh cover over his hips and legs, both for warmth and for modesty. It took all her strength to not stare at his muscular body. It struck her that even injured the man looked powerful and strong.

"Hendry," she whispered, dipping a cloth in cold water and dabbing it gently across his face. His skin was cool, his color still too pale. "Ye must awaken."

She tried again. And again.

Cool water. A soft shake. Her voice, rising with urgency. "Hendry, ye must open yer eyes!"

At last, his eyelids fluttered, lashes twitching before lifting just enough to reveal hazy, unfocused blue eyes. He looked at her with a furrowed brow, a faint moan escaping his lips.

Relief washed over Ailith.

"Ye must stay awake," she urged, touching his cheek. His eyes began to drift shut again, and she gave him a firmer shake. "Do ye hear me, Hendry?"

A breath. Then, "Aye," he rasped.

Her shoulders lowered as she studied him and reached to touch the side of his neck. His pulse was steady, and the bleeding on his side had finally staunched. The worst might be behind them.

Now all she could do was tend his wound and pray the man she once loved would still be himself when he woke fully.

The contrast of his bright blue eyes to his almost black hair was arresting, and even more so, as he quietly regarded her as she administered to his head wound. Without any additional bandages, all she could do was wash out the wound. The next day, she would inspect it and see about perhaps stitching it closed if need be.

He'd fallen asleep, and she worried that he'd not wake.

Deciding it was best to stay close and waken him regularly, she set about dragging the slumbering man to her bedchamber.

"Come, Teller, we have another laborious task to complete before eating."

# CHAPTER THREE

THE INSISTENT POUNDING of his head was hard to bear. Hendry refused to open his eyes, fearful that light would make things worse. The surroundings were silent, and the scents that permeated were unfamiliar. He was not at the keep; he was sure of it.

The aroma of food made his stomach growl.

As he adjusted himself on the blankets he lay upon, he winced when his side protested. By the pull of the skin, he'd been wounded and then stitched. The fact that he'd been cared for hopefully meant he'd not been taken by the attackers.

Slowly the memory formed of him returning from his parents and being attacked by three men. A dagger had cut his right side and one of them had driven a blade through his left side. That is where his recollection stopped.

By the way his head pounded, Hendry was sure he'd been struck from behind. A direct blow to the head. It was a miracle they'd not made sure he was dead before leaving. If not for the damn pulsing of his head, he would smile because one memory that remained was that of the men's faces. It wouldn't take much to find them.

Needing to know where he was, or at the very least get the layout of his surroundings, Hendry forced his eyelids up. Just a bit. There was nothing. He was in a modest bedchamber. On the floor, next to him was a small, neatly made bed, with only a tattered blanket on it. He scanned all along the walls for hints of where he was, but there were scant belongings. Only a trunk at the foot of the bed, and a small table upon which a candlestick was the sole item.

He took several deep breaths and pushed up to sit. The threadbare blankets that had somehow managed to keep him warm slid down from his chest and pooled on his lap. He was naked, not one stitch of clothing on his body. Fortunately, his head pains didn't increase. Unfortunately, they didn't decrease either.

It couldn't be helped; he'd have to seek out who'd nursed him and thank them. Once dressed, he'd ride to the keep. The sooner he and the guard went after the attackers, the better.

He got to his feet and swayed a bit, but not enough to be worrisome. Not bothering to cover himself, as he was sure it had to be a lone male who'd managed to drag him into the room, he went in search of his clothing.

"I wish to thank ye for yer help…" He stopped speaking at seeing Ailith by the hearth stirring a pot. On instinct his hands flattened across his private area.

Her eyes flew to him, sliding down his body, hesitating for a moment on his bandaged midsection before dropping lower. Instantly realizing just where her eyes had fallen, her cheeks reddened, and her eyes flew to his. "Yer clothes are folded next to where ye lay. Did ye not see them?"

Once standing, he'd not looked to the side by the wall, not wishing to turn his head more than necessary.

"I-I didnae." He turned to go and swayed again.

"Wait." Ailith rushed to him. "I am nae sure ye should be

upright yet. Yer head wound is very large and deep. It is a wonder ye survived."

Although she was diminutive next to him, he allowed her to place his arm over her shoulders and lead him back into the bedchamber.

Once there, she pointed to the bed. "Sit."

He did as he was told and cupped his hands between his legs. "Thank ye for all ye did for me. I can get dressed."

Ailith nodded, her gaze searched his face, concentrating on his eyes. "Today is the third day since ye came to my door. Ye have been unconscious for most of the time."

So this was the third day since the attack. He had to get to the keep. "I will dress and ride home. I am surprised no one has come in search of me."

"No one has come." She shrugged. "Where were ye traveling from?"

"My parents' home."

Her hazel eyes slid to look away from him. "They must assume ye decided to extend yer visit."

It was true, he often remained a sennight when visiting. This time he'd cut the visit short because they planned a gathering that would include matchmaking. Not in the mood to indulge his parents' fantasy that he marry a local woman and return to live there, he'd decided to leave.

She let out a breath, and her expression hardened. "Get dressed, then ye will eat. If ye are sure to be able to ride, then it's best ye go."

"It must have been hard not to let me die," he said as if he was teasing, but there was truth behind his words, and she knew it. "I ken how ye feel about me. Would prefer if I had died in Brant's place."

Ailith's gaze bore into him. "I dinnae wish anyone to have died. Once ye are dressed, I expect ye to leave immediately," she said and practically ran from the room.

Dressing was a tedious process, each movement seemed to increase the headache, and he prayed it would ease. His tunic had been hemmed and everything was washed, giving him pause. So strange that although Ailith claimed to not like him, she'd not only cared for his wounds and given him shelter but she'd taken the time to mend and wash his clothing. Women were hard to understand.

When he finally emerged, the front room was empty. Save for a bowl of stew and flat bread left on the table, there was no other signs of Ailith or her dog.

He ignored the food, knowing she was losing a meal in order to feed him. Since his purse had been stolen, he'd return another time to compensate Ailith. He'd bring coin and food once he was able to retrieve more from the coffer in his bedchamber at the keep.

His horse stood contentedly in the clearing, tail flicking lazily from side to side as it grazed on the lush, dew-sweet grasses. When Hendry approached, the beast lifted its head and gave a soft neigh of recognition and trotted closer. Upon reaching Hendry, the animal gave him a gentle nudge of its velvety nose against his cheek, as if checking he was still in one piece. There was comfort in that simple gesture, a small flicker of familiarity amidst the confusion of two days lost.

To his relief, the saddle was already secured. Whether Ailith had done so before she left, or the horse had remained saddled the entire time, he couldn't say. Either way, he silently thanked the woman for the kindness.

Climbing onto the horse was a brutal endeavor. His skull throbbed with every movement, the pain radiating behind his eyes like an ax buried in his brain. Worse still was the wound along his side, hot and unforgiving. Reminding him that battle wounds never traveled kindly. He'd ridden hurt before, but the agony never got any easier. Each jolt in the saddle a cruel reminder that he was far from healed.

Once astride, he turned his gaze to the cottage and scanned the edge of the woods beyond it. No sign of Ailith. The absence gnawed at him. She was out there somewhere, foraging for herbs, burdened with a basket, all while danger in the way of bandits and those who saw lone women as prey.

His jaw tightened. It wasn't just concern. It was something deeper. Something raw and protective.

Uttering a soft expletive, he guided the mount toward the thicket of trees, making slow progress. Not just because the path was barely clear, but because any movement made him want to curse loudly.

It wasn't long before he saw her, with her faithful dog by her side, both by a creek drinking. The animal reacted first, lifting its head and turning to look. His menacing growl immediately alerting Ailith, who remained crouched, looking around until she spotted him.

Unsure why, he lifted a hand in greeting. When she didn't return the gesture, he lowered it feeling dumb.

She placed a hand on the snarling dog's back. "Stop Teller," came the stern order, as she walked toward him, basket dangling from her arm.

"Why are ye here? Ye should be on yer way."

As much as he wanted to dismount, he wasn't sure he'd be able to climb back into the saddle if he did. So he peered down at her. "Ye should nae be out and about. I was attacked and left for dead. I can nae imagine what they would do if they caught ye alone."

Her eyes shifted toward the cottage. "Unlike ye. I have nae choice. Herbs are how I am able to feed myself and Teller. I must also come out and check my snares for rabbits and such." When she wiped away the hair from her wet face, she huffed. "Go on now. Be on yer way. Dinnae worry yerself. I have survived here alone and will continue to do so."

It was on the tip of his tongue to remind her of when he'd happened upon the cottage and found her fevered and barely coherent. Instead he nodded. "I will wait until ye return back and ensure ye are safely inside."

Her jaw tightened, and he almost smiled at the fiery lass. She had to be the most self-sustaining woman he'd ever known. Too proud to accept help or cede defeat, she would fight for survival.

Finally she nodded. "Do as ye wish but dinnae expect me to hurry because of ye. If ye fall from the steed, I will leave ye where ye lay."

"I dinnae believe ye will," he replied.

With a huff, she turned on her heel and marched toward a thicket. The dog looked up at him as if questioning his reluctance to leave, then turned and trotted after his master.

True to form, as he expected, it was perhaps another hour before Ailith was satisfied to have gathered enough and return home.

If she knew the time had helped Hendry's head clear, she

would have probably not lingered as much. By the time the door to her cottage slammed shut, except for a twinge here and there, his headache was practically gone.

Upon riding into the keep's courtyard, he was immediately greeted by his squire, Tobin, who held the horse's reins as he dismounted with difficulty.

"Are ye injured sir?" Tobin's eyes scanned over him, the protective lad's expression troubled. "Ye dinnae look well."

He handed the scabbard and sword to the lad glad to have the weight off his back. "Nothing to worry about. Nothing that won't heal with a hearty meal and rest."

Not looking satisfied, Tobin motioned for a stable lad to come and get his steed. Then walked alongside Hendry as he made his way to the front entrance of the keep. In silence they entered the dim interior, and Hendry waited a bit for his eyes to become accustomed before proceeding forward.

Once in the great room, he went to the table usually reserved for the warriors and lowered slowly to sit.

Tobin must have made some sort of motion, because immediately a serving lass neared and placed a tankard of ale before him.

"I will fetch ye a meal," she whispered and hurried away.

It was but a moment later that he was joined by Liam, whose brows rose while studying him. "Ye are nae well my friend."

Indeed it was a struggle to keep his eyes open, but he refused to go anywhere until eating.

Thankfully before Liam could say more, the serving lass returned with a bowl piled high with meat chunks and potatoes in a thick hardy broth. She placed the bowl in front of him, and a basket with rolls next to it.

Liam reached out and took the lass's wrist. "How fare ye, Josefina?"

The lass's eyes rounded, and she pulled her arm out of his grasp. "I am well, sir. Do ye wish to be served?"

Though not at his best, Hendry could tell something had transpired between the two.

"Eat with me," Liam said, seeming as though he wished to speak to the pretty lass. But Josefina just glanced down and didn't respond.

"Just ale," he told the lass, who went to the sideboard and retrieved a tankard and pitcher. Her cheeks flushed under Liam's scrutiny as she poured the ale. Her jaw set, she didn't spare him a glance.

"Thank ye," Liam told the lass, who turned and hurried away.

"Whatever ye did, I dinnae think she has forgiven ye," Hendry said.

Liam glanced in the direction Josefina had gone and grunted. "What happened to ye?"

"I was attacked. Three men. It seems they have a practiced way of ambushing. Two come out and have a go at ye on two sides and whilst ye are distracted fending them off, a third comes from behind."

A muscle flexed on Liam's jawline. "It has to be the same ones that have been attacking others. Ye should nae have ridden alone."

"I was returning from my parents' home. Warriors dinnae require escort. We must warn everyone about this."

His friend's brow lowered. "Did this happen today?"

"Nae, two days ago."

"Where have ye been?" It was Laird Alexander who asked as he neared. "Did ye recover alone in the forest?"

Hendry went on to tell them about regaining consciousness at Ailith's cottage and how the woman had cared for him. He explained that she didn't have much but had done her best to bandage his wound.

Alexander lowered to sit next to him. The powerful build of the warrior reminding Hendry of why he'd worked so hard to emulate the laird until gaining the same expertise and form.

Hendry ate his fill and answered questions between bites until Alexander placed a hand on his shoulder and told him, "The healer will be here shortly. Until then, go to the bathing room and wash off so that he can tend to yer wounds. Warriors will be sent in search of the thieves."

"About Ailith…" Hendry began. "I need to send her recompense and some food. It is best if she does nae leave her cottage until it is safe."

"Send yer squire with whatever provisions ye wish. He will be escorted." Alexander met his gaze for a moment. "The lass may nae accept anything from us."

"Then give her no choice," Hendry replied.

BY THE TIME the healer was done, his wounds had been cleansed and bandages replaced. The other injury on the back of his head had also been thoroughly washed and the healer had stitched it closed after picking out dried blood. His head was now wrapped, the tightness of the bandage somehow relieving any discomfort.

Although Ailith had done her best, she only had so much clean bandaging. She had done what she could redressing his wounds with the freshly washed cloths to keep dirt and dried blood away from his open wounds.

"The infection is nae spread. Ye should heal shortly," the healer informed him. "Head wounds are worrisome, but it seems ye have made it past the time to expect any lingering troubles."

Once left alone in his bedchamber, Hendry looked up to the ceiling. He wanted to get from the bed, to take the provisions to Ailith himself. All he could manage was to inhale and exhale, his body sinking into the bedding.

After two knocks, Tomin entered carrying Hendry's scabbard and sword. He pulled the blade and showed it to Hendry. "I have cleaned it and polished it for ye," the lad explained.

"Ye did very well," Hendry told him. "I have a task for ye. Ye will go to visit the widow, Ailith, and bring her the provisions I tell ye to. Ye will be provided with an escort. Dinnae go alone."

The squire nodded, his eyes bright at the prospect of fulfilling such an important task.

# CHAPTER FOUR

Ailith studied the flames in the hearth; her mind constantly going to Hendry. Why was he back in her life? It seemed that either on purpose or by happenstance, the warrior was showing up too often in her life.

It had been difficult not to think about the *what ifs* and recall their past time together when he'd been there, in her home. The picture of his body kept reappearing in her head. And as much as she tried to push the images away, her mind ignored it.

There had been a deep and abiding love between them. Then she'd married another. Ailith got to her feet and added a log to the fire though it really didn't need it. She had to keep busy, not idly sitting about giving free rein to her thoughts.

Teller, who'd been dozing by the fire, stood and stretched, then went to the back door, scratching it with his large paw.

Since Hendry's attack, she'd been wary of straying too far from the cottage. It was best to be within running distance in case those terrible men returned. They'd been very close to her home and may have noticed smoke from her chimney. If that was the case, it was possible they'd come to find out who lived there.

"Out ye go," Ailith told the obedient dog, holding the door open. She stood in the opening, eyes scanning the dark woods.

Thankfully the moon was full, so she was able to track Teller as he sniffed the ground, searching for the perfect place to relieve himself.

Later in bed, she stared up at the roof, sleep unable to come. Every sound outside made her jump, and she had already checked to ensure both doors were barred securely twice.

TELLER'S BARKS WOKE her the next morning and she sat up groggy from lack of sleep. She threw on a skirt, tucked her nightshift into it, and left the bedchamber to quiet the dog.

Peering through a hole in the window covering, she noted that a young man on horseback rode toward the cottage. He was escorted by two fearsome warriors, who constantly scanned the area.

What were the laird's guard doing there?

Suddenly her stomach plummeted. Had they come to inform her that Hendry had died? Or perhaps to inquire if he was there after he'd not managed to make it to the keep?

Ailith hurried to the door and flung it open. Teller rushed out and stood in front of her baring his teeth.

The lad hesitated to dismount until Ailith touched Teller's head. "Down, Teller." Teller lowered to sit, his wary gaze on the visitors.

The young man neared, his eyes moving from her to Teller. "Are ye Ailith?"

"Aye," she replied.

"I am Sir Hendry's squire, Tobin. He sent me to bring ye these items." He motioned to the warriors who'd dismounted. Each held a large sack that they carried toward the door.

"Wh-what is this?" she stuttered. "What are ye doing?"

One of the warriors slid a look to her. "I dinnae ken what is in here," he replied gruffly, brushing past to put the heavy burden just inside the door while she gaped at the audacity of the man, not bothering to ask if he could enter.

The second guard did the same, though with a bored expression. Upon walking from inside her cottage, his gaze roamed over her, more with curiosity than interest.

Tobin held out a small sack and placed it in her palm. "He asked that I tell ye he wishes to ensure ye are well provided for and have little need to venture far from the cottage." He smiled down at her dog, who wagged his tail, seeming to ken the lad was harmless.

The squire turned to the warriors who were mounting. "The shorter one is my uncle," he said with pride.

The warrior motioned to Tobin. "Come along. Dinnae linger. We have duties to perform."

Tobin leaned and patted Teller's head. "Take care, Mistress Ailith." With that, he hurried back to the horse, mounted gracefully, and the trio turned their horses and galloped away. Teller racing after them, barking with excitement.

Speechless, Ailith shook her head. It was then she realized she still held her hand out, with the sack of coins in it.

"What just happened?" she asked Teller, who ran back, tongue hanging out of the side of his mouth, his face bright with joy at having performed a duty.

As dogs do, Teller couldn't care less. Instead he trotted to the side of the house to find the garden water tub.

She went back inside and looked at the bundles. She opened one and gasped. Inside were a pair of thick blankets, two large sections of fabric, two wooden bowls, a small pot, and two goblets. It was an interesting assortment of items, she considered.

Now very curious, she went to the second sack, which had been placed on the table, and pulled it open. She was shocked by the bounty she found. Inside were potatoes, carrots, and onions. Wrapped separately was a loaf of crusty bread, a small block of cheese, and dried sausage. In two other bundles were a choice section of pork and a portion of beef. And lastly, there was a wineskin filled to almost bursting. It was truly a bounty like she'd not had in years.

Although she didn't want to accept the items, it would be impossible to return it all. She didn't own a mule or a wagon. Both had been sold long ago for much-needed coin for food and such.

The sack of coins was the last thing she opened. He'd given her more than enough coin that she'd be able to purchase food for an entire season. That was the one thing she'd not accept.

THE AROMA OF the cooking made Ailith swoon with anticipation. She grew a few vegetables in her garden, which rarely made it to full ripeness. Now that she had food that she could preserve and eat, it would allow her garden time to flourish.

In a broken clay jar she'd found, Ailith set some freshly picked flowers on her table. After rinsing one of the new bowls, she served up a meal of roasted carrots, savory meat, and just a bit of the bread. She then spooned some of the stew into a small clay pot, she used to feed Teller.

Once seated, she looked at her meal and, without warning, tears slipped down her face. Despite her pride and still not caring for Clan Ross, the meal and other provisions were a blessing. One that came at a time she barely any resources left.

The food was wonderful. Ailith had seconds and sopped up the last of the meat juices with the delicious bread and finished it with a half cup of the sweet wine.

THE NEXT DAY, Ailith was cutting the softer fabric to make a chemise and a simple shift dress. With the other fabric, a wool, she had enough to make a skirt and blouse that would keep her warm when venturing out.

Once she finished the task of cutting, she planned to sit by the door, taking advantage of sunlight and fresh air as she sewed.

After stopping only once to eat, the morning went by quickly. Already she'd finished the chemise and was starting on the shift dress when Teller alerted her that someone was coming.

Ailith quickly grabbed her sewing and retreated into the cottage, calling Teller to come inside.

Once the door was firmly latched, she peeked out through the hole in the curtain and saw her sister's husband, Boyd, coming up in their horse-drawn wagon. Next to him was her sister, Erin, holding the youngest of their four. As they pulled closer, Ailith opened the door, and she from the noise level she could tell the other three in the back were ready to be set free.

It was a whirlwind of activity as the family climbed from the wagon, the father helping the children and then hoisting a sack upon his shoulder. Her sister was the first to reach her, baby in her arms and two-year-old grasping her skirts. The two older, both boys, raced around the cottage playing with a delighted Teller.

After depositing the sack inside on the table, Boyd grabbed the toddler and went back out to keep an eye on the boys.

"Peas, beans and oats," her sister said by way of greeting as she pulled a blanket from a chair and placed it on the floor, then settled the sleeping infant on top of it. "Ye can make a hearty pottage that will last ye for a few days."

Ailith filled two glasses with cool well water, placed one in front of Erin, and took the second one to Boyd.

"I am so grateful that ye always look out for me. I must admit to having more than enough food at the moment. Please take it back to feed yer bairns."

Erin waved her protests away. "It is only a small portion of what we got after Boyd's work at the Macdonald farm. The farmer is a very generous man. Each of the four workers received good compensation along with their pick of the crop."

"That is quite generous indeed," Ailith agreed.

Erin looked at the sleeping child. "That blanket is new. Did ye make it?"

The sisters never kept secrets from one another. Erin was privy to all that had occurred when she'd chosen to marry Brant over Hendry. Her sister had been against the marriage and had never warmed up to her late husband. Despite Ailith explaining that Hendry was not being faithful, Erin refused to believe it, claiming Brant had lied in order for Ailith to agree to marry him.

Over their three years of marriage, if ever doubts or

thoughts that perhaps Erin was right crossed her mind, Ailith pushed them away.

She took a deep breath. "I found Hendry just outside the door. He was badly injured and unconscious. I dinnae understand how he managed to get here."

Erin gasped. "What happened? Is he alive?"

"Aye, he recovered. Although I must admit to fearing many times that he would not. Once he was well enough to leave, three days later, he left immediately." Ailith ignored her sister's pointed look. "I insisted he leave."

"I am sure ye were nae the friendliest," Erin countered. "I ken ye continue to unfairly blame him and the others for Brant's death."

Deciding not to begin the familiar discussion Ailith said, "He sent quite a bounty as recompense. Food, blankets, and fabrics. Also some coin."

"Ye must keep everything," Erin said in a stern tone. Her sister knew her too well. "Ye deserve every bit of it since ye refused to accept the widow's allocation from the laird."

It was true. At the time of Brant's death, Ailith had been filled with bitterness and sadness. Her mourning had not only been for the loss of her husband, but she had also been terrified of the future. With no parents and her sister not having room for her, she knew the path ahead would be a lonely one.

"I am nae sure about keeping the coin." Her words rang hollow. It would be idiotic to return the money. With winter approaching, she'd need every cent for oil and food.

"Did ye talk to him? Ask him what the truth was?" The warmth in her sister's gaze was like an embrace. Yet, she pressed the issue about her ire with Hendry further.

Ailith ignored the question. "Tell me about what happens in the village? I have nae been able to go. First, Teller hurt his paw; then, caring for Hendry, the days have passed quickly."

Knowing she was evading the subject, Erin didn't repeat her question, which surprised Ailith. "There was a brawl at the village square. The hothead Cormac as usual, but this time with one of the laird's warriors. One called Liam."

Ailith knew both men and didn't have to ask to ken Liam had probably overtaken Cormac, who lacked fighting skills and relied on brute strength. "Liam won."

"Aye," Erin laughed, the hearty sound making Ailith smile. "Cormac wrapped his arms around Liam's chest, holding him up from the ground. Then Liam hit Cormac in the face with his elbow until Cormac fell like a tree."

"Cormac needs a good lass to settle him down," Ailith mused. "A strong lass will calm that temper of his."

"I dinnae believe it is a bad temper, but more that he likes to fight," her sister explained.

"Possibly," Ailith said. "What else? How is Mairi?" she asked, referring to Erin's mother-in-law, who lived with them.

Erin looked to the doorway and lowered her voice. "A constant bother. Is nae satisfied with anything I do, cook, or say." Erin shook her head. "She fell in the garden the other day and although I was inside, she claimed it was my fault."

Both giggled, the subject of Boyd's difficult mother always fodder for their conversations. Her sister dug into her skirts and extracted a small pouch. "Three coins for the herbs that were purchased. I sold plenty of eggs this time as well."

"I plan to go to the village in the next few days. I have

herbs that will be ready very soon," Ailith informed her sister.

The family remained until the sun was low in the sky and had to leave so as not to travel in the dark. Erin stood in the doorway watching them until they disappeared from view. As always, a few tears trailed down her cheeks. She loved their visits but immediately missed having them there. If she were to have one wish, it would be to live near her sister.

She sewed by candlelight until her eyes drooped, only to be awakened by Teller's low growl. Someone was creeping about outside.

Heart thundering, Ailith grabbed the only knife she owned. Her eyes trained on the front door.

Then she took Teller by the scruff and dragged the still growling dog into her bedchamber. It wouldn't keep her safe for long if someone managed to get inside, but at least it would offer another barrier between her and whoever it was.

At first, she considered it could simply be an animal outside. Perhaps a wild boar searching for food. But then the unmistakable sound of a man's murmur caused her to flatten against the door. Whoever it was didn't try very hard to get inside. Instead, they seemed to hesitate when Teller growled and barked menacingly.

Although whoever it was had left soon after Teller had alerted her, it was dawn before Ailith finally allowed herself to fall into an exhausted slumber. Even then she jerked awake and breathless at every sound.

# CHAPTER FIVE

After three days abed, Hendry was beyond glad to finally be able to move about without his head feeling like a drum being pounded. He went to the great room and walked to the table where his team of warriors sat. Every eye followed his progress, measuring his movements, gauging whether he was fit for duty.

It wasn't malicious on their part. Hendry understood that more than anything, he and his men were like brothers, each of them integral in keeping one another safe. As much as he wanted to reassure them he was fit, he would never lie to his men. He was able to ride and keep up, but if there were any kind of fighting required, he would be of little help.

Upon arriving, each man greeted him warmly. One of them, a thick muscled, red-haired guard, called Rory, gave him a once over. "If ye aim to ride today, I will go with ye. Stay by yer side," the man said in his usual gruff, no-nonsense tone.

Hendry gave the man a nod. "I will ride today, so it would be helpful."

To keep things normal, Hendry asked the men for reports on their progress to catch the men who attacked him and other occurrences they may have come across during their patrols.

As frustrating as it was that the attackers were adept at

hiding, in a way he was glad. Because now he could take part in their apprehension. See their expressions when they realized he was alive.

As he made his way to his bedchamber to fetch his overcoat, a young maid called Una was walking out carrying a bucket and broom.

"I have tidied yer bedchamber," she informed him, giving him a flirty smile. Una put the bucket down and leaned the broom against the wall. Then she walked closer, lifted her hand and leisurely ran her finger down the side of his face. "Is there anything else I can do for ye?"

She'd warmed his bed a time or two, but it had been many months since the last time. Obviously, she'd lost interest in her latest conquest.

Hendry smiled down at the pretty lass. "Ye never change Una. Always playful and always bonny."

Her face brightened at the compliment. "'Tis my nature, I suppose." She hesitated and studied him, her head cocking to the side. "Something is different about ye." A burrow formed between her brows. "Some lass has yer attention. Am I correct?"

At first he was going to deny that someone indeed had his attention. However, it would be the best way to avoid another assignation with Una. Despite enjoying her company and witty banter, he wasn't prepared for another round of her dramatic antics.

"I will not deny it," he replied, noting her eyes narrowing. "Is it Lily? The lass in the kitchen? Every man in the keep seems to be going out of his way to speak to her. She is frigid and doesn't seem the least bit interested in men, I'll have ye ken."

"Who?" Hendry asked, genuinely perplexed. "I dinnae believe to have met her. It is nae someone within the keep." Not wishing to continue the conversation, Hendry brushed past the now sullen Una and walked into his bedchamber to retrieve what he needed.

ON PATROL, RORY did as he'd promised. Riding alongside, not hovering, but close enough that if Hendry started to fall, he'd catch him before he hit the ground.

There were four others ahead a short distance away, and another four keeping their distance behind. The last six men had traveled in the opposite direction with repeated descriptions of the men they hoped to find.

"We've patrolled the shorelines and the border villages and gone to the southern areas and to the western areas without any success," Rory informed him.

"Has anyone gone to Tokavaig?" Hendry asked. How was it possible for the three men to be able to hide so easily? In all possibility, the men had been seen by one of his men, but they'd not recognized them.

Rory scanned the surroundings, always alert. Hendry continuously kept watch as well, his gaze moving from side to side.

"Let us ride to the village," Hendry called out to the men in front. Those in back would follow their trail.

Despite giving him an obvious look of someone wondering if he'd lost his mind, Rory remained quiet.

BY THE TIME they reached the village, Hendry wondered if he'd be able to ride back. Every jolt of the horse had tugged at the stitches along his side. The skin around the wound now burning with every breath. A warm trickle had begun to seep beneath his tunic, sticky and slow; an ominous sign that some of the stitches had likely split.

The dismount was agony. He gritted his teeth, swaying slightly before his boots found purchase on solid ground. But standing upright brought a grim sort of relief. A stable boy approached and took the reins without a word. Hendry gave him a curt nod of thanks, glad for one less burden. The healer's cottage would have to be his next stop, if he didn't pass out in the middle of the square first.

The village was bustling, the market in full bloom. The air carried the mingled scents of roasted meat, fresh bread, and crushed herbs. People moved about briskly: bartering, gossiping, living.

Hendry raised a hand to one of his guards walking behind him.

"Have the others stay on the outskirts as we walk through," he said low but firm. "I dinnae want to frighten those we seek into hiding."

The man nodded and peeled away, heading to relay the order.

He motioned for another guard. "Spread out. Check the tavern and the shops. Look for any who match the descriptions I gave."

When he began walking, Rory held back, giving him space. Perhaps to lend Hendry the appearance of a harmless villager, which was not believable with his muscular build and sword across his back, or maybe just out of respect for his pride.

Hendry scanned the crowd, eyes narrowing as he swept the

faces of the men first, instinct guiding him like a hound on a scent. Then he saw her.

Ailith.

She stood at a small herb stand, speaking to two women, her light brown hair catching sunlight like threads of shadowy silk. Her booth was simple yet charming, adorned with vines twisted into an arch over two slim poles made from young trees, freshly stripped of bark. Bundles of herbs hung in fragrant bunches from the greenery, dancing gently in the breeze like forest charms. On the makeshift counter, small sachets and embroidered squares lay in neat rows. He squinted.

Was that the fabric he'd sent her?

She wore a new dress, soft, simple, but clearly fashioned with care. A shift of pale blue, cinched at the waist, the stitching neat and deliberate. A curious warmth stirred in his chest. Was it pride? Satisfaction? Whatever it was, it settled like a balm easing some of the ache in his side. She'd taken what he gave and turned it into something beautiful. Something *hers*.

She turned suddenly, brows drawing together as if sensing eyes on her. Her gaze swept the market, searching.

Then their eyes met.

Her lips parted in surprise, just barely. The flicker of disbelief that crossed her face was quickly masked. But it was enough. She hadn't expected to see him. Likely, she thought he was still abed, convalescing like a sensible man.

He supposed she'd agree with Rory: there was no good reason for him to be out riding so soon after being wounded.

And yet, here he was, drawn to her like a moth to the flame.

One foot in front of the other, he walked toward her.

AILITH DID HER best to ignore the man moving through the crowd toward her, unfortunately, her eyes refused to listen and often strayed up noting each movement. For a tall muscular man, he moved fluidly, like a wolf stalking its prey.

"Just these." An elderly woman placed a coin in her palm, bringing Ailith back to the business at hand.

Another person, did the same, grabbing the last of the embroidered handkerchiefs. The income from the sale would be enough to buy leftover portions of fabric and thread to make more and then still have a few coins left.

Her last customer bought a bundle of herbs, inquired about when she'd bring more handkerchiefs, and to her chagrin, left just as Hendry neared.

His blue eyes met hers, and he nodded in greeting. The contrast of his dark hair, olive complexion, and bright blue eyes were what had first attracted her to him. The first time they'd met had actually been there in the village. She'd walked out of the bakery and bumped into him, dropping her basket. Despite her protests that her bread was unharmed, he'd purchased her another loaf. Afterwards, he'd walked with her about the square, asking question after question about her. It was the first time a man had shown such interest in her, actually holding a conversation rather than spending the time recalling his own exploits.

"Do ye walk here?" he asked, his gaze moving to the herbs and then to Teller, who sat behind her on a straw pallet.

"That is the only way to get here," Ailith replied curtly. "Is it not too soon for ye to be out riding?"

He slid a glance past her, scanning the surroundings. "I am the only one who can recognize the men who attacked me. The sooner we find them, the better." Hendry scratched the stubble on his jaw. "Ye should nae be walking here on yer own. It is dangerous right now."

"How am I to live then? How will I make a living and purchase things I require? It is out of necessity that I come to the village." For some reason the statement made her stomach clench. Hendry had never been in her situation. His family lived a comfortable life, and he'd gone from there to living at the keep, always having good meals and enough coin to purchase fine clothing.

"I understand, which is why I made sure that ye have enough provision to last until we capture the renegades. A woman alone is easy prey."

Ailith turned away to greet a customer who purchased the last two bundles of herbs. The day was turning out to be a good one, she was sold out.

"I will take ye back," Hendry announced, his stern expression leaving no room for argument.

"Ye will nae," Ailith stated. "Teller and I will return on our own, when I decide to leave."

Once again he scanned the surrounding, his sharp gaze hesitating every so often. Always a warrior, always aware of his surroundings.

He turned to look behind him, then back to her. "One of

my men can take the dog. Ye will ride with me."

The last thing she wanted was to be pressed against him, immediately being reminded of his body, how he'd remained toned and firm.

Rising to her tip toes, she leaned forward, lifting her face to glare up at him. "I said nae. I dinnae wish for more from ye. Ye have done more than enough to repay my caring for ye. If I am to be honest, the only reason I kept the lot was because I never received my widow's portion. Still, I am undecided about keeping the coins."

"Is that so?" His right brow rose. It was as if the infuriating man was amused. "What I sent is not enough for saving my life. I ken ye dinnae care for me in the least."

"I never said that." Ailith stated, cringing that she'd spoken the words. Refusing to be the first to look away, she narrowed her eyes. "Be on yer way warrior."

His mouth pressed against hers. It was a soft quick kiss, but nevertheless a kiss. He straightened, seeming as shocked as she was, but he quickly regained his composure and took a step back. On the other hand, Ailith was frozen to the spot.

A wide shoulder lifted and lowered. "I will wait for ye by the bakery."

He knew she'd purchase bread before leaving the village. Ailith let out a huff. "Ye can wait all ye want. I will nae go with ye."

"Aye, ye will."

IT WAS ALMOST absurd, the image of the hardened warrior Rory perched stiffly cradling a wide-eyed Teller on the saddle as they rode.

She scanned the surroundings, doing her best to keep from relaxing into Hendry's body.

Ailith held herself ramrod straight, not just out of aversion of the closeness, but because Hendry hadn't the strength to bear her weight. Every step of the horse jostled his injured frame, and she could feel the slight tremble in his muscles as he struggled to remain upright behind her.

Four warriors emerged from the woods, their horses falling into step. Other than a flicker of curiosity, none addressed her.

"We didnae spot anyone matching the descriptions," one called out to Hendry. "But a man at the pub claims he saw them two nights past."

"They rented a room for the night. Just one room," added another.

"Likely on yer coin," Rory muttered with a dry chuckle as he steadied Teller, who squirmed wanting to be put down.

Hendry let out a grunt that might have passed for a curse. "They're still on the isle, then."

They pressed on in silence, broken only by the occasional groan Hendry couldn't quite suppress. Each soft sound made her chest tighten. She twisted her head to look at him, her brow arched in disapproval.

"I can walk from here," she said quietly. "My cottage is just beyond those trees. Ye need to rest, not play the martyr."

To her surprise, he didn't argue. His gaze dropped, heavy-lidded and exhausted, and he gave a curt nod. "Rory, we'll stop here."

One of the warriors dismounted and came to help her down, his hands gentle but efficient as he guided her to the ground. He then went to retrieve Teller, who wiggled, impatient to be put on the ground.

Ailith reached for the sack tied to the saddle, but her hand collided with another. Hendry's. His fingers closed over hers.

"Be with care," he murmured, his voice low and rough.

A jolt of awareness raced up her arm. Their eyes locked. His were clouded with pain, but there was something else there too, something far more dangerous. Familiar. Longing.

She yanked her hand away, lifting the sack with a defiant tug. "Try not to fall off the horse," she muttered. "I doubt yer pride could take another blow."

He let out a tired huff that might have been a laugh.

She turned away quickly. She could not afford to soften.

Years ago, she'd given her heart to Hendry McNichol, and he'd shattered it like glass underfoot. She'd refused to allow him into her life ever again. He'd proven not to be trusted with her heart.

Hendry had gone to another isle, without coming to see her and when she'd gone to search him out, a warrior called Brant had told her, in a voice laced with pity, that Hendry had taken another to his bed the night before leaving.

It had been a servant girl called Una, with whom he'd often slept with. Brant had even called on his squire, who'd confirmed what the warrior had said.

She'd cried for many nights. Sleep had become a stranger. Food an afterthought. Her days had passed in a haze of silent agony, and her nights were filled with cold, empty silence.

She would not go through that again.

No matter the flicker in his eyes.

No matter the warmth of his hand.

No matter how much her heart wanted to remember the

way he once looked at her.

She would not let the wall she'd built crumble. Not for him.

# CHAPTER SIX

HENDRY REFUSED TO remain idle. Restless and still sore, he ignored the dull ache in his side and strode out to the training field, his boots crunching on the hardened earth. Sword practice echoed across the grounds, metal clashing, warriors grunting, and barked commands piercing the air. The familiar rhythm of drills brought a measure of calm to his unsettled mind.

Liam stepped up beside him, arms crossed, his gaze trained on the line of archers loosing arrows at straw targets. The steady *thwack* of shafts hitting their marks filled the air.

"Ye are looking better," Liam remarked, cutting a glance at him. "Still pale as a corpse, though."

Hendry smirked. "And ye look like one who lost a wager and got dragged behind his horse."

Liam's bruised jaw and swollen eye told the tale. Purple bloomed across one cheekbone, and the corner of his lip was split. Still, he didn't flinch from the jab.

"Cormac was cruel to a young lad," Liam muttered, his voice low and tight. "I'll nae stand for that, especially if it's someone who cannae defend himself."

Hendry nodded, his respect for his friend deepening. "I heard. I'd have done the same. Cormac's as dense as stone. A knock to the head might actually help."

Liam chuckled, then winced and touched his side. "Aye, worth even the aching ribs."

The two of them stood in silence, the cool breeze stirring the scent of sweat, leather, and the faint iron tang of sharpening blades. But Hendry's thoughts weren't on drills or bruised egos. As the sun climbed toward its descent, unease bloomed inside him.

The patrol should return soon.

He prayed they'd come bearing news, and prisoners. Every hour that passed gave the attackers more time to vanish into the forests, or worse, escape the isle altogether. Despite the border patrols, the wild terrain of Skye was riddled with hidden paths, and the mainland was only just over a day's ride away.

By the time the sun hovered low in the sky, casting a golden haze over the compound, the returning riders appeared on the horizon. Their massive warhorses trotted in, eager for rest and feed, snorting and pawing the earth as squires rushed forward prepared to take the reins and the warrior's weapons to clean.

But there were no prisoners in tow.

Hendry's chest tightened. The look in the men's eyes told him everything. Faces drawn, jaws clenched, disappointment and something darker etched in every line. He strode toward the warrior he'd placed in charge, his voice clipped. "What happened?"

The man's expression turned grim. "We found a man. Wounded. Beaten the same way as ye. He died before we reached his home, but he was able to give us a description of the ones who did it."

Hendry's breath caught. The warrior didn't need to elaborate. The image was clear: blood, desperation, a final whisper of justice before a family's world was shattered. That grief, raw and consuming, would follow them for many months, if not years.

Word spread quickly. Hendry joined the patrol in reporting to the laird.

Inside the great hall, tension crackled in the air as they recounted the news. Laird Alexander Ross, normally calm and composed, surged to his feet. Fury carved deep into his features, his hand slamming onto the table with such force that goblets rattled and the room fell instantly silent.

"At dawn," the laird's voice thundered, "the entire force rides out. Every mile of Ross land will be searched. Every croft, every barn, every crumbling ruin. No corner left unturned."

He paused, his next words seething with righteous wrath.

"We will find the cowards. And make them pay."

A roar of agreement erupted in the hall. Blades were unsheathed and raised high, the warriors chanting as one, voices rough with fury and justice.

"*Death to them! Death to them!*"

The cry echoed like a war drum, a storm gathering on the horizon. And Hendry stood among them, his pain forgotten, his blood humming with the promise of retribution.

The moment the warriors' chants echoed through the hall Hendry's thoughts flew to *her*.

Ailith.

His chest tightened painfully. Would the bastards, cornered and desperate, stumble upon her secluded cottage? Would they see her simple home as the perfect place to hide?

To take what they needed?

To hurt her?

The thought sliced through him sharper than any blade. He pressed a hand to the edge of the table, steadying himself, though no one seemed to notice he was quiet.

He was a warrior. A commander. Duty demanded he ride at dawn, lead the full force of their might to flush out the murderers.

But Ailith, *his Ailith,* was alone. Vulnerable. And no matter how he tried to bury the truth, he couldn't deny the pull in his chest. He loved her. Still.

As platters of roasted meat and trenchers of warm bread were passed down the long tables, Hendry sat stiffly among his comrades. The hall buzzed with the hum of anticipation, warriors murmuring about their plans. Which direction they'd ride. How they'd gut the traitors if given the chance. There was pride in their voices, excitement at the justice to come.

But the noise washed over him like a distant tide.

He couldn't hear them. Not truly.

All he could see was Ailith. Her beautiful hazel eyes filled with fear. Her arms wrapped around that shaggy dog. The fragile peace she clung to out in that woodland cottage and how easily it could be shattered.

He had to act.

Rising from the bench with sudden resolve, he barely registered the turned heads. "Going to see my squire. I'll return shortly."

A few nods. A shrug. The others turned back to their meal and spirited talk of vengeance.

Hendry strode from the great hall, his pace brisk, his heart thudding with urgency. He searched the kitchens first. Empty, but for a few lingering servants who informed him Tobin had already eaten. Without pause, he turned toward the courtyard.

The soft clink of metal on stone led him to the blacksmith's hut, where Tobin stood beneath the silvering sky, oiling a sword. The squire's face lit up at the sight of him.

"I brushed down yer horse and sharpened yer blade."

"That's not why I came," Hendry cut in, his voice firm, low.

Tobin blinked, straightening.

"Tell me, Tobin… have ye kept up with yer sword training?"

The lad's chest puffed with pride. "Aye, sir. Daily. With Cynden and his first," he said, referring to the laird's youngest brother, who was in charge of training the squires and younger guard force.

Hendry gave a tight nod. Good. That made what he was about to say easier.

"Then I've a task for ye. One I dinnae give lightly." His eyes locked with the young man's. "It's a matter of life and death. And I'm trusting ye to guard something… someone… I could nae bear if she were to be hurt or worse."

Tobin's face sobered, all youthful bravado vanishing as he stood straighter.

"Of course, sir," he said.

AILITH BENT LOW among the rows of her croft garden, her fingers brushing aside damp earth as she reached for a cluster of broad beans, their pods swollen and heavy with promise. A few leeks stood tall and proud nearby. While cabbages, large and pale green, glistened with dew in the morning light. She plucked each vegetable with care, brushing the soil from their roots with practiced movements. This harvest, while modest, was hard-won. She had planted everything in stages, thinking ahead, so she wouldn't starve before spring's thaw.

But she remembered too well the lean ends of winter, when her cupboard held only dried peas and the occasional tough squirrel or hare snared in the woods. Hunger had a memory. And it haunted her.

A sudden, low growl from Teller froze her in place.

Her heart leapt, a cold rush of fear replacing the warmth of the morning sun. She straightened sharply, her breath catching in her throat as she scanned the edge of the forest beyond the garden. Teller stood alert, hackles raised, eyes locked on something just beyond the trees.

Then she saw it. Movement. A rider, still distant, blurred by light and shadow.

Her pulse quickened. She clutched Teller's scruff and backed toward the cottage, nearly stumbling as she turned and rushed through the door. Slamming it shut behind her, she leaned against the wood, her chest rising and falling as a wave of dread crested in her chest. Her hands trembled, and tears stung her eyes. It was becoming too much, living with the constant shadow of fear, never knowing if the next stranger would be the last thing she saw.

Moments passed. Then came a knock.

Teller launched into frantic barking, his body rigid with alert.

Ailith's breath caught again. She crept toward the door, each step slow and deliberate, as if a wrong movement might shatter the fragile barrier between her and whomever waited outside.

A voice called through the din. Young. Not aggressive.

"Miss Ailith, I am Tobin, squire to Sir Hendry. I come at his bequest."

She quieted Teller with a sharp command, hand still pressed to the door as her racing heart fought for calm. The boy's voice came again, firmer this time.

"I come to ensure yer protection."

Unlatching the door, she cracked it open, peering out to find a young man with a sincere expression and wind-tossed hair.

"Why would he send ye?" she asked, relief and confusion warring within her.

Tobin's shoulders lifted in a shrug. "The men who attacked him have killed a man. Hendry believes they may try to hide in these woods. He fears ye may be at risk."

She blinked at him, taken aback. "Wh-why would he send *ye*? I can bar my doors. There's no need for concern. Surely ye have duties far more important than watching over me."

Tobin's brows dipped, his youthful face hardening. "There is nae duty more important than protecting a clanswoman."

His words struck something deep inside her. She wanted to argue, to insist she didn't belong, not truly. But she did. Her family had lived on Skye for generations. Her blood ran with the roots of this land. To deny it would be a lie.

And she was tired of living like a shadow in her own home.

"Very well," she murmured, finally relenting. "What do ye require?"

A grin broke over Tobin's face, boyish and bright. "I've all I need. I'll build a fire and camp over there." He pointed to a patch of grass near the grouping of trees to the east. "Looks to be a fine spot. I would ask permission to draw from yer well, to water the horse, and for myself."

"Of course," she said softly, her gaze drifting to his mount. The animal stood patiently, laden with a bedroll, a pair of sacks, a bow with a quiver of arrows, and a broad sword. The young squire was clearly prepared for any danger that could come.

Once Tobin set about his tasks, she returned to the garden. But everything felt different.

The weight in her chest had lifted. The shadows no longer reached quite so far. She still glanced toward the trees now and then, but no longer with dread. With Teller close and the young man keeping watch, she could finally breathe, really breathe, for the first time in days.

And that small, fleeting feeling of safety? It felt like sunlight breaking through a storm.

LATER THAT DAY, she invited Tobin inside for last meal. He agreed, bringing with him his weapons, which he deposited just inside the door. Perhaps because she'd met him before when he'd brought provisions, Ailith was comfortable around him.

When she placed a bowl of leek soup with small chunks of meat in front of him, Tobin's eyes widened. "It smells delicious," he said.

Ailith put a basket of freshly baked bread and a small pot of butter on the table and sat down with her own bowl. "Aye, it was my mum's recipe. My sister and I make it all the time. Helps us feel closer to her."

As they ate, she was able to garner that Tobin was an orphan whose parents had been killed during the MacLeod raids when he was but ten and two. Hendry had happened upon him when he'd been digging for food from a farmer's garden. The warrior had not chastised him but had taken him back to where he was camped for the night and shared his food with the boy. Then he'd taken him back to the keep to live.

"I have nae had an empty belly since," Tobin finished his tale with a grin. "Sir Hendry, he has treated me better than my own da, who often beat me."

It was easy to believe in Hendry's kindness, especially when it came to the boy. It seemed that he'd treated Tobin with the gentle authority of a man who understood being that age, lost and hungry for belonging. And that was what made the betrayal cut twice as deep. The man she had come to love had always shown kindness to everyone… so how could he have been so careless with her heart?

"Whoever he marries will be a fortunate woman," Ailith said, her tone light and casual, though her words held the weight of an unspoken need to know more about Hendry's current life. She stole a glance at Tobin, hoping for answers he might not realize he was giving.

The lad nodded as he chewed, not the least bit suspicious. "If he ever courts one, I suppose he will one day. Hendry has nae courted a woman since I've known him."

Her breath caught. "Truly?" she asked, feigning mild interest, masking the surge of emotion that rushed through her. "That is surprising. Most of the laird's warriors are reputed to be charming scoundrels, at least until marriage tames them." She added a soft laugh, meant to keep things light, though she wasn't sure it sounded the least bit true.

But Tobin's attention drifted. The curiosity that had sparked her line of questioning dulled as he turned the topic. Asking instead about her life in the cottage, about Teller and how she'd come to care for the pup.

She told him the tale, how a kindly old villager had gifted her the scrappy creature, the runt of a litter found in the woods. Her voice grew warm as she described Teller's first days with her. How he'd shivered against her side and barked at falling leaves. As she spoke, Tobin's eyelids drooped, his full belly and the crackle of the fire pulling him into drowsiness.

"I think ye should sleep while ye can," she suggested gently, her heart softening as he looked so young when drowsy. "Come nightfall, ye'll need yer strength if we're to keep watch through the night. Bring yer bedding in here, next to the hearth. There's no need to build another fire just yet."

The lad shook his head, rubbing his eyes. "Nay, I'll set it up outside. I prefer it. But wake me before ye turn in for the night, aye?" He stretched with a yawn. "Thank ye for the fine meal, Ailith."

She smiled as he stepped outside, Teller following close behind expecting an adventure.

Hours passed in quiet peace. The room dimmed, shadows stretching long. Sleep tugged at Ailith's limbs. She peeked through the door, the wooden hinges creaking softly. Tobin sat on a fallen tree, hunched near the fire, its glow painting his face in flickering gold. He spotted her and raised a hand; she returned the gesture, a small smile on her lips.

At least he was warm, she thought. Her own bedchamber lacked a hearth and with winter still a whisper on the wind, she hadn't yet moved to sleeping in the front room. Until the cold came fully, she'd continue heating stones by the fire and tucking them under her blankets.

She lay down, the bed cool beneath her. Sleep crept in slowly, but her thoughts clung stubbornly to Hendry.

Why hadn't he married?

Could it truly be, as Tobin claimed, that she'd been the last woman he'd courted?

Squires knew everything, their master's moods, their secrets, even the women they fancied. She wanted to believe it, wanted to think she'd mattered to him in ways no other had. But it seemed too hard a truth to cradle without it breaking apart.

Teller let out a grumbling sigh in his sleep, a soft, sleepy protest. She reached out, fingers brushing over his coarse fur, her touch gentle, calming. A smile curved her lips.

"Loyal beast," she whispered, her voice barely a breath. "Ye'd never leave me."

# CHAPTER SEVEN

Mounted in front of the entire Ross army, flanked by the other leads and just behind their laird, Hendry couldn't keep from admiring the perfectly lined up warriors, archers, and guardsmen.

Every face was taut with expectation. Across their backs and on their hips, weapons capable of bringing death to the enemy. There was little doubt that the cowards they sought would be captured.

From where he was, to the laird's left, he caught sight of Alexander's set jaw as his keen gaze traveled over his men.

He'd known Alexander and his brothers since they were all lads. They'd played in the forest whilst their mothers traveled between their homes visiting. It seemed now those peaceful happy times as a child where he'd mostly known safety were fleeting. He also now understood that the reason he'd felt secure was because of the sacrifices of men like him. Warriors.

"Remain vigilant," Alexander called out upon finishing his speech. As always, he spoke in a way that made the men sit straighter, shoulders squared, knowing they make their laird proud.

The warriors broke apart into ten teams. Each team consisting of twenty warriors, six archers, and two scouts.

Hendry guided his horse forward planning to go to his

team but stopped at Alexander holding an arm out to stop him.

The laird's emerald green gaze was direct, no hint of what the man was to say. "It will be upon ye to decide their punishment. Ye have time to consider it as ye go with yer men."

Usually punishment was dealt by the laird, but Hendry understood that after being close to death, Alexander would grant him this. Despite all they'd done, and having taken lives in battle, deciding a man's final fate beforehand was not easy task.

However did Alexander do it, when required? Making such a decision weighed heavily on a man.

Hendry nodded. "Thank ye Laird."

"Dinnae thank me. The decision could be a burden."

"I am aware," Hendry replied, leaning over to place his hand on Alexander's shoulder. "Nonetheless, I do appreciate yer confidence in me."

AT MIDDAY, HENDRY and his men dismounted near a babbling creek, the sound of the water moving through the rocks too tempting to pass by. They led their thirsty horses to the water's edge, and the men drank alongside their mounts.

Some men sat on the ground, others lay flat resting their backs, still others wandered the forest intent on finding any sign of those they sought.

Hendry and his men were about to mount when the unmistakable sounds of horses approaching got everyone's attention. It was Liam and a few of his men, riding toward them at a leisurely pace.

It wasn't like his friend to break away from his group and

even rarer still for his approach to be so casual.

Upon arriving, Liam and his companions dismounted. Like Hendry and his men they took their mounts to the creek's edge. One of them took Liam's horse as the archer walked to Hendry, pulling him aside.

"We've got yer men. I am sure of it. They are just as ye described. One of them still has yer leather purse, the one with yer initials on it." Liam blew air through his nose. "The bastards had the nerve to say we could nae prove it. They believe ye dead."

It took effort to force a smile as Hendry patted his friend's shoulder. "Yer men are to be commended."

Liam's shoulder lifted and lowered. "'Tis the scouts who do most of the work. The rest of us do the battling and the killing."

At the statement, Hendry had to laugh. "True, vera true." He looked toward the road. "Where are they?"

"Being brought. We rode ahead to find ye. Already one of my men has turned back to tell them ye and yers are here."

Despite the fact that everyone, including Ailith, would be safer, Hendry didn't look forward to dealing out their sentence.

If it was the right ones Liam's men had captured, and he was sure they had, then he'd have to make a very hard decision. Not only give sentence but be witness to his orders being followed.

"Something weighs heavy on yer mind?" Liam asked, his keen gaze meeting Hendry's. "What is it?"

He had to swallow past the dryness in his throat. "Alexander has decreed that I am to decide on the punishment for them."

Liam's eyes widened and shook his head seeming to understand how Hendry must feel. "Have ye thought on it?"

"I have thought of little else," Hendry replied. "Their death will make the families of their victims feel vindicated, for that I am glad."

The screech of an owl sounded in the nearby trees. The piercing sound declaring it had found its prey. It was almost as if nature sent a message. Every living being must live according to a code. When the balance was offset, there was a price to pay.

It wasn't long before Liam's men crested the hill and rode toward where Hendry and his men were. Liam turned to him. "I have every reason to think this is them. They tried to escape upon seeing us, throwing items into thickets. I ordered my men to look for whatever they tried to get rid of. I expect it to be items that will tie them to the attacks."

The trio were bound to saddles on very tired and gaunt horses. They'd obviously not been cared for. Despite the men's bloody noses and split lips, Hendry felt worse for the horses.

It was obvious by their open mouths and wide eyes that they'd never expected to see him alive. Much less standing before them as they were yanked from the horses and made to kneel before him.

"Is this them?" Liam asked loudly as their men formed a circle and looked on.

One by one, he met each of the men's gazes, noting no sign of remorse. Instead they sneered as if daring him to say something against them.

"Aye," Hendry replied loudly.

"See that the mounts are watered before ye head to the keep," Liam called out and met Hendry's gaze as the horses with their prisoners were taken toward the creek.

"I will send men to inform the relatives of those harmed. They will wish to be there to see the trio punished." His friend hesitated for a moment. "Take time to yerself. Alexander will expect a decision upon yer return."

"I am going to fetch Tobin. The ride will give me time alone to think," Henry said, looking toward the creek where the gaunt horses drank their fill. "Their horses will benefit from all this. One can tell if a man is honorable by the way they treat their animals. There is no honor in any of them."

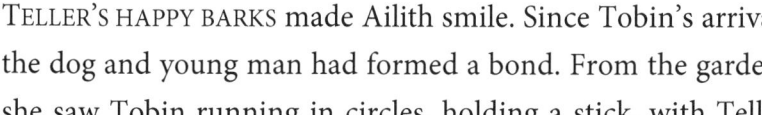

TELLER'S HAPPY BARKS made Ailith smile. Since Tobin's arrival, the dog and young man had formed a bond. From the garden, she saw Tobin running in circles, holding a stick, with Teller chasing him. When he threw the stick, her dog dashed after it and returned, dropping at Tobin's feet.

It was obvious the young man had a heart for dogs, and Ailith wondered if he had one of his own. She imagined life at the keep provided little rest, but at the same time a dog would be a relief from the doldrums of each day.

Both Tobin and Teller walked to the rain troth, and she watched as he dipped the dog's bowl into the water and placed it on the ground, before dipping the cup that hung from twine taking some for himself.

"I will miss him," Tobin said softly, reaching down to scratch behind Teller's ears. The dog leaned into the touch, tongue lolling in bliss. "I best go walk about and ensure all is well."

"Be with care," Ailith stated. "I best go inside then."

Tobin gave a crooked smile and tilted his head toward the road. "I will, but ye can remain outside. And as fate would have it, here comes my master himself."

Her stomach gave a traitorous flip. She turned to see a rider approaching, the thud of hooves rhythmic and steady. Before she could speak, Teller took off in a flurry of excited barks, tearing across the path and nipping at the horse's legs with wild abandon.

"Teller!" Ailith called, her voice sharp. The rider pulled his mount to a halt and dismounted in one fluid motion.

Then something changed.

The dog's stance softened, hackles lowering as he sniffed the man's boots and cloak. Within seconds, Teller's tail was wagging furiously, and he was circling Hendry like an old friend returned from war.

"Traitor," Ailith muttered beneath her breath.

Tobin chuckled, a low, warm sound. "Yer dog's becoming friendlier. He'll be wanting belly rubs from the next intruder that crosses yer path. I fear that may be my fault."

She gave him a sidelong glance. "He'll snap back into guardian mode once ye and Hendry leave. I've always believed dogs can sense cruelty and those who carry none."

Then Hendry stepped fully into view, and her breath caught. Dressed in worn leather and thick wool, his hooded cloak dusted with road and wind looking every bit an intimidating warrior. The sword strapped across his back spoke of danger; the shadows in his hazel eyes, of things he'd seen and done.

Ailith swallowed, unsure of the fluttering in her chest. It seemed more a foreboding sense that she was about to tread dangerous waters.

Hendry neared greeting Ailith with a slight nod. "Ailith, how fare ye?"

"I am well," she replied automatically, looking him over for any sign of pain or distress. It seemed that in just a few short days, he'd made almost a complete recovery by the smooth way he moved and walked.

"Tobin, ye are free to return to the keep. Ensure to bathe and get rest. Ye can return to yer duties the day after tomorrow."

The squire turned to Ailith. "Be with care."

"Ye as well," Ailith replied, watching as Tobin hurried away, Teller racing after him with a stick in his mouth.

"Teller will be disappointed at losing the attention Tobin gave him," Ailith said, a hint of sadness slipping into her tone.

Of course the young lad would be glad to return to his own bed and not sleep in the cold every night. Still, she was selfish in having enjoyed the company and sense of security at night.

"The men have been captured. There is nae need for ye to be worried that they will return here."

Hendry's statement made her look up into his eyes. "I am glad. Surely the laird will nae go easy when doling out their punishment."

The reaction that her words caused was unexpected. Hendry closed his eyes and let out a breath before nodding. "Do ye care to go for a walk? I have need to stretch my legs."

It was on the tip of her tongue to decline, but at the same

time, she wanted to know what had caused his reaction to her statement about the assailant's punishment.

They were quiet as they made their way along a narrow path that she often used when foraging for herbs. Their footfalls crushing twigs and fallen leaves causing birds to burst from bushes and fly in unison to a higher haven. Their loud chirps announcing their displeasure.

"Ye are fortunate to live in such a peaceful place," Hendry said, hands down his sides as he walked beside her. "I am nae sure that I would be content without seeing others at least daily."

Ailith let out a breath. "Although I have very little choice in the matter, as it was the home where Brant and I lived, I do enjoy the solitude. I must admit to being lonely most days, however."

Annoyed at herself for sharing, Ailith pressed her lips shut vowing to not repeat the mistake again. "Ye live inside the keep then?"

Hendry shook his head. "I live in one of the cottages near the stables. I prefer not to be inside the main house where there are always servants and visitors underfoot. I only go there to meet with the laird and for meals."

Not knowing very much about his current life was strange given how they'd both professed their love for one another in the past. Now it was as if he'd become a new person. A guarded man whose tones and expressions revealed very little about what he thought.

Though, perhaps because in the past she had known him so well, Ailith could see past the front he put up, past the façade he presented. She knew no matter how unbothered he appeared, something burdened him. Something was pressing on his mind.

"What is it, Hendry? Something troubles ye greatly." Ailith gave him a pointed look. "And dinnae lie to me and say there is nae on yer mind."

He stopped walking and nodded. "If I am to be honest, ye are the first person I considered talking to. Perhaps because at one time, ye were my advisor and always guided me so well."

The last thing she wanted to think about was the past. The way they'd talked late into the night, whenever able to steal away. They'd developed a relationship where they'd spoken freely, without fear of judgement. They often gave each other advice, or if it was warranted, comfort.

"Whatever it is, ye can tell me," Ailith said quietly, within her there was a warring of sentimentalities. On one hand, she would help anyone even those she didn't care for. On the other, she feared he was chipping away at the protective wall she'd so painstakingly built. Warnings rang wildly inside every part of her being.

He lifted his head and met her gaze. Whatever troubled him was grave indeed.

"The laird has decreed that I will be the one who decides what their punishment is to be. Although I have battled many times, have taken lives, it has always been because I am defending my own life, or that of others. I have never had to decide of how it is to be carried out. To end a life…" he finished quietly.

As he ran both hands down his face in what seemed to be exhaustion, Ailith considered how to reply.

"It is best to think of the families of the people who suffered under their hand. Though it's harder to think of yerself, since as a warrior ye put yer life on the line all the time. Ye should think of yerself. If not for making it to my cottage, ye would be dead. How would yer family feel then? Would yer parents blame themselves for nae having insisted ye stay longer? Otherwise, ye would have avoided the danger. What those men did deserves punishment, and they nothing less than what they did to others."

Hendry kept his gaze forward, the only sign he'd heard her was a slight nod. So Ailith continued, "This is nae a time for guilt. It is a time to be glad for them being captured. A time to have pride in that ye and yer men are keeping the clans' people safe."

Once again, he nodded, but this time his shoulders visibly relaxed. "Yer words. The way ye say things has always helped me get through hard situations."

When he spoke, it was as if the years apart melted away, as if they'd not been living separate lives all this time. Immediately she wanted to flee, to get away from him and how tempting it was to slip back into a life in which Hendry was a large part.

"We should return. Any moment now Teller will come rushing to find me." She turned, not waiting for Hendry to respond, then stopped when his hand curled around her upper arm.

"We should talk," Hendry said in a quiet voice. "I need to ken the truth, the real reason for what happened between us."

At once her heart began thundering. What could she say that he didn't already know? It wouldn't solve anything to dredge up these old wounds. There was nothing he could say that would make things better.

Ailith looked up into his eyes. The sincerity was obvious, but there was something deeper as well. It was the look he gave her just before declaring his love. How could a man who claimed to love her, was then unfaithful, and had not sought her upon his return, expect explanations from her now?

The cruel truth clung to her like a second skin. Despite everything, her heart still ached for him. Forgiveness wasn't a choice; it was a demand. Hendry had always held her soul in the palm of his calloused hand, even when she tried to will it back. Yes, she had loved Brant, but it had been gentle, kind... safe. What she felt for Hendry was nothing less than ruinous. A love that consumed.

That burned.

They moved toward each other as if drawn by an invisible thread, pulled by something older than memory, stronger than reason. Their mouths met in a clash of heat and longing, lips melding with an urgency that stole her breath. Her arms slid around his neck, fingers threading through the thick strands of his hair, anchoring herself to the only man who had ever undone her with a single glance.

He groaned into the kiss, deep and raw, pulling her hard against him. The rigid planes of his chest pressed against her softness, his body a furnace of want. His hand cradled the back of her head while his tongue claimed her mouth, sweeping it with hunger, tasting her like a man starved of both sustenance and hope.

The kiss shattered every wall she'd built. Her pulse pounded in her ears. Her breath hitched with every press of his lips. She moaned, a soft, involuntary sound, when his hand slid along her spine, pressing her closer, tighter still. Heat bloomed low in her belly, spreading like wildfire through her limbs.

Hendry was the only man who'd ever made her feel this way, like her skin was too tight, like her heart was trying to beat its way out of her chest. Her knees weakened and her body trembled beneath the onslaught of sensations.

Then his hand found her breast.

Ailith gasped, head falling back as his fingers teased the peak through the fabric, then beneath it. Her moan was soft but desperate, laced with disbelief that this was real. That he was here. Touching her like this. Loving her.

His mouth left hers and trailed down her neck, tongue drawing heated circles just beneath her jaw. At the same time, his thumb teased her nipple, mimicking the rhythm of his tongue, coaxing her body to arch into him with a will of its own.

She wrapped an arm around his waist, hand splaying across the muscles of his back. Gods, he felt the same…strong and solid and maddeningly perfect. Memories flooded in. His bare skin beneath her touch was the temptation she'd resisted when she'd bathed him. Though every inch of him had begged to be kissed.

This time, she wouldn't resist.

When his mouth found her breast, taking the stiffened peak between his lips, a cry escaped her. Half whisper. Half plea. "Hendry…"

At the sound of his name, he growled low in his throat, a sound that slid down her spine and set her trembling. His tongue worked its wicked magic. Swirling. Teasing. Drawing her deeper into a haze of ecstasy.

Everything else disappeared. The world around them

ceased to exist. There were no trees, no wind, no sky.

Only him.

Only the man who had once broken her heart, and was now making it beat again with wild, aching need.

And she wanted nothing more.

WHEN HENDRY FINALLY pulled back, he gently readjusted her blouse and held her by the shoulders, his touch trembling with restraint. Ailith stood dazed, chest rising and falling in uneven breaths. Heart thundering like hooves on stone.

"Wh-what..." she whispered, her mind fogged from the searing heat that had just passed between them. Her gaze lingered on his lips, kiss-swollen and trembling with words he hadn't yet spoken.

But she didn't hear him. Her own pulse roared too loudly in her ears.

"I'm sorry, what did ye say?" she finally asked, voice barely above a breath.

"I cannae do this," Hendry said, his voice rough. "Not until I ken why did ye nae wait for me?"

The question hit her like a slap. Cold, cruel, and cutting.

Her breath caught. "What?" she whispered, then louder, angrier. "What?"

Emotion surged like a wave, dousing the warmth between them. Her heart twisted as disbelief turned to fury.

"How dare ye ask me that?" Her voice shook with wounded rage. "After what ye did, ye have the audacity to question my loyalty?"

His brows knit, confusion flickering across his face. "What do ye think I did?"

"I dinnae think, Hendry, I ken." Her laugh was bitter, sharp. "I was told what ye were doing while apart from me. Taking maids to yer bed. Other women. Regularly."

His face hardened, lips pressing into a tight line. But she couldn't look away, not from the rise and fall of his chest, not from the hurt gathering in his stormy eyes.

"And ye believed it," he said, quietly. "After everything. Ye believed I'd betray what we had."

"Ye expected I wouldn't find out?" she challenged, crossing her arms even as her throat tightened.

"And yet," he pressed, stepping forward, "ye didn't come to me. Didn't ask if it were true. Ye took the word of some whispering tongue over the man who loved ye beyond sense or salvation."

"I didnae want to believe it…" Her voice cracked. "But it made too much sense. Ye never sought me out before ye left or after ye returned. Ye vanished."

"I returned," Hendry said, his voice rising with frustration, "to find out ye'd married Brant. No warning. No explanation. What was I meant to do? Was I to chase after a married woman?"

"To explain!" she shot back. "Ye owed me that!"

"How was I to ken that ye thought the worst of me? I didnae understand what happened?"

For a moment she couldn't speak. Had Brant lied?

His expression turned to anguish, then anger. "And when he died, ye turned cold. Bitter. Full of blame. And still I ensured ye had what ye needed to survive. I never stopped looking after ye, even when ye could barely stand to look at me."

"I didnae want yer charity," she spat. "He died because of the Ross clan, because of yer battles! And I was left alone!"

Hendry's voice dropped, low and deadly. "Are ye angry because ye're alone… or because ye still love me and cannae forgive yerself for it?"

The words gutted her. She inhaled sharply, eyes stinging.

He stepped closer, his voice like a blade now, tempered and honed. "A warrior's duty is to defeat the enemy. We protect our kin when we can, even at the cost of our own lives at times. Ye weren't there, Ailith. Ye didn't see what happened. The men who fought beside Brant mourned him. They wept. They bled. And they loved him like a brother."

His gaze pierced her. "But ye? Ye turned grief into hatred and flung it at those who didn't deserve it. At me. And I wonder, do ye grieve him at all? Or do ye simply need someone to blame so ye can bury what ye really feel?"

She stumbled back, as if he'd struck her. The words left her stripped, raw and exposed.

Hendry's expression shifted, horror creeping across his face at what he'd just said. His hands dropped from her shoulders as if burned.

"It's best I go," he said hoarsely. "There's nothing left for me to say."

And just like that, he turned, leaving her standing in the ruins of what might have been. Her heart torn between truth, grief, and the terrible ache of still loving the man who'd just broken her all over again.

She stood frozen, her hands balled at her sides, fingernails biting into her palms, but the pain was a distant echo compared to the storm inside her. Brant had lied to her. Of that she no longer had any doubt. Because what Hendry had said was right. She knew him better than any other person and just then he'd not lied. Every word he'd spoken was the truth.

All these years she'd accused him of betrayal, to every person who asked she'd repeated the same thing. Had somehow convinced herself with each repetition that it was true. That she had been right in marrying Brant.

Why? Because it was the only way to avoid the truth that she'd always known. Hendry had never betrayed her. It was the other way around.

It was she that had betrayed him. It was she who'd been unfaithful. *All the blame was on her.*

Hendry turned away.

And with every step he took, it felt as if pieces of her were being torn loose and carried with him.

She wanted to call out. To demand he stop. To take back every cruel word. No. Not take them back, but to explain them. So many years of resentment, loss, and heartbreak were tangled between them like thorn-covered vines. But she couldn't speak past the knot in her throat.

Her legs gave out at the heaviness that overtook her.

Ailith crumpled to her knees, the grass damp beneath her skirts, her arms wrapping around herself as if she could hold in the heartbreak trying to spill out of her chest. Her breath came in ragged gasps. Tears streaming freely down her cheeks, falling to the earth with a quiet patter.

"It was me," she whispered, voice shaking. "Ye have always been honorable."

Through the years she'd built walls high enough to cage dragons. Walls of anger. Of pride. Of pain. And he'd broken through them all with a kiss, a question, and a single look of disappointment in his eyes. That was what shattered her the most. He still looked at her as if she mattered.

But she hadn't believed in him.

Not when it counted.

She pressed her forehead to the ground, breath hitching as a sob escaped. How many lies had she swallowed just to survive? About what he felt. About what she felt. About how none of it mattered anymore.

She heard the faint crunch of his footsteps fading, swallowed by wind and distance. He wasn't running. He was walking away like a man who'd given his final battle everything and lost.

And she let him go because in her heart she knew he would never forgive her. Even if he did, there wasn't a future for them. It was finally the true end between them.

The ache in her chest burned hotter than any desire. It was the ache of words unspoken, of time wasted, of love still alive but buried under grief and doubt.

Ailith lifted her head, tear-streaked and trembling, and whispered into the silence he left behind.

"I never stopped loving ye."

She looked up, noting he was gone.

And this time, she as sure he'd never return.

A black blur came into sight. Teller rushed toward her, ecstatic at having found her. The dog's tail wagged furiously as he neared and licked the salty tears from her face. Then he sat on his haunches and leaned into her.

There in the forest, Ailith hugged her only source of comfort and cried and cried.

# CHAPTER EIGHT

Hendry dismounted with a curt nod to Tobin, handing over the reins without a word. His boots scraped against the stone of the courtyard, echoing like judgment in his ears. The sound of life around the keep, voices, footsteps, even laughter all felt strangely hollow. As if the world hadn't noticed something inside him had cracked open and begun to bleed.

He didn't speak or look at anyone.

With shoulders tight and fists clenched, he stalked to his small cottage that was tucked just far enough from the main hall to be left alone. Once inside, he shut the door with more force than needed and slid the latch into place.

Cold met him like an unwelcome hand on his skin.

No fire glowed in the hearth. Of course not, Tobin had been away. The air was damp and still. Somehow more silent than the world outside, as if the walls themselves refused to offer comfort.

He crossed the room, pulling out a chair at the worn wooden table and dropped into it like a man whose bones had turned to stone. Reaching for the half-full bottle of whiskey, he didn't bother with a cup. No ceremony. No pretense. Just pain. Drinking straight from the bottle, he let the burn sear its way down his throat. It settled hot and hollow in his belly like everything else inside him.

Another swallow. Then another.

Finally, he set the bottle down with a dull thud and just sat there, staring blankly into nothing. His vision blurred, not with tears, but with the haze of exhaustion that comes when a man has carried too much for too long. Outside, life continued: boots scraping, the clang of practice swords, the rise and fall of voices.

But inside his home, time had stopped.

This was a day of endings.

Three men would die at dawn, their crimes unforgivable, their fates sealed. And Hendry…he would be the one to see it done. He had already chosen the manner.

Hanging.

Not quick. Not clean. It was fitting.

A slow, gasping death.

It was what it had felt like, walking away from Ailith.

That same choking sensation. As if his lungs had collapsed, and his soul had been sucked out through the wound she'd left behind. He'd thought himself hardened after all these years. But seeing her again, touching her, tasting her, had brought everything back.

Only he wasn't able to lose himself in her. He'd asked the question he'd been wanting to ask, and her reply had shattered something he didn't know was still breakable.

She'd believed the worst. That he would betray her. That his love, which had burned for her through every day of absence, could be so easily sullied.

He took another drink, the whiskey now dulling the sharpest edges of memory.

He remembered the day he returned. He'd been tired. Yes. But hopeful. Ready to see her. His mind had played the scene a hundred times. A thousand times.

He'd bathed, changed into clean clothes, and prepared to ride out and find her. His heart had beaten like a war drum in anticipation of being with the one he loved.

But fate had a cruel sense of humor.

Liam had pulled him aside. The archer's usual easy grin was gone, replaced by something taut and nervous. Hendry had assumed someone, perhaps one of his parents, had died.

"Hendry..." Liam had said quietly, voice lined with sorrow. "I dinnae ken how to tell ye. Ailith... she married Brant. A fortnight past."

The words hadn't made sense at first. Not to his ears. Not to his heart. It was like being struck in the chest but feeling nothing until the breath refused to come.

He didn't remember leaving the keep. Only the feel of the reins in his hands. The rhythmic clop of hooves. The path through the forest. He remembered seeing Brant first, standing outside the cottage. Then Ailith had stepped out, her gown catching the sun like spun gold.

They stood together. Close. Familiar.

And when Brant pulled her into him... when she leaned her head against his shoulder... Hendry's world unraveled.

He didn't confront them. He couldn't. His mouth wouldn't have been able to form words and deep inside, he understood that his soul couldn't bear to hear any explanations.

Instead, he'd turned and ridden off without a destination, grief pressing against him from all sides like a crushing wall of rocks.

Finally, it was his horse that had chosen the destination, and somehow, they ended up at his parents' door.

They'd said nothing at first. They didn't need to.

Just Ailith's name had been enough. His mother's arms, loving and comforting, his father's silence, solid and unyielding, had held him steady while the ground gave way beneath him. He stayed there until the ache dulled enough to breathe again. Until the pain reshaped itself into a man he no longer recognized. Until Hendry McNichol became something harder. Sharper. A blade instead of a heart.

And now, all these years later, he found himself in the same place again. Still bleeding for her.

Still loving her.

And she still didn't believe in him.

He closed his eyes and leaned back in the chair, head tilted toward the ceiling, bottle once again in hand.

"I would've given ye everything," he whispered into the dark.

But the silence only answered with the sound of his own breath.

And the slow, steady ticking of time that would not turn back.

THE LATCH GAVE a soft click.

Hendry didn't move.

The door creaked open behind him, cold air drifting in before it was shut with a quiet thud. A pause. Then the shuffle of boots across the wooden floor.

Liam lowered to a chair across from him. He said nothing, but his presence pressed gently against the edges of Hendry's sorrow like balm on a burn.

The silence between them stretched, filled only with the pop of the cork as Hendry opened the bottle again and took another long swallow.

Hendry didn't look at him. Just stared at the ceiling. "We are meant to be resting. We ride early to the village."

"Aye," Liam said simply.

A few heartbeats passed.

"The burden of the sentence is a weight ye must bear knowing it is a just punishment from what they've done," Liam said, assuming the reason for his glumness.

He tried and failed to say something about what awaited in the morning. In truth, he'd accepted it. Swallowing, he said. "I have accepted it."

"Then something else burdens ye. It is Ailith?"

The words landed like a blade drawn gently, not to wound, but to acknowledge that the pain existed.

Hendry swallowed, jaw tightening. His voice was hoarse when it came. "Aye."

"Ye look like a man gutted."

"I feel worse."

He sat back and let the bottle rest on the table between them, then dropped his head into one hand, elbow braced on the worn wood. The fire still hadn't been lit. He didn't want it. Let the cold in. Let it numb him.

"I waited for her," he murmured. "Even when I tried not to. And all this time, she thought I…" His voice broke, not with tears but with bitterness. "She thought I'd betrayed her. Believed it without question. That's what cuts through me."

Liam didn't offer comfort. Didn't try to soothe or soften it. That was what Hendry liked about his friend. He didnae mistake silence for weakness.

Instead, Liam spoke truth.

"Ye have never stopped loving her. Have given way to the belief that one day ye and her will be together. Sometimes, my friend, certain things are nae meant to be. It may be time ye accept it."

Hendry let out a quiet, humorless laugh. "I dinnae think I have any option but to move forward. I have wasted too many years pining over a woman who didnae believe in me."

Liam offered the ghost of a smile but said nothing more.

The room settled again. Still no fire. Just the bitter cold creeping in, and the shared silence of two men who understood pain better than they should.

After a long stretch, Liam rose and walked to the hearth. He hesitated, then quietly struck flint to steel and sparked a flame to life.

Hendry didn't stop him.

The fire began to glow, casting flickers of amber light across the stone walls. Shadows danced across Liam's face, softening the hard lines carved by years of battles and the hardship of a warrior's life.

After a moment, his friend took a few steps, lingered at the door, then turned back. "Get some rest, Hendry. Even if it's the kind that only whiskey grants. We will head to the village directly after first meal."

With that, his friend walked out, the sound of the door closing seeming loud.

And Hendry remained, staring into the growing flame.

He didn't cry. Men like him had long since spent their tears.

But deep within himself, something cracked.

# CHAPTER NINE

A BITING WIND cut through the village square. The kind of wind that sliced between cloak folds and settled deep in yer bone. Ailith drew her cloak tighter, the wool coarse beneath her fingers, but grateful for anything to anchor her against the chill, *the one in the air, and the one inside her.*

She hadn't meant to come. Hadn't planned to watch men be led to their deaths. But when Erin's husband came to fetch her, she hadn't refused. She couldn't. Not because she hungered for justice, or vengeance, or the grim finality of the gallows, but because she needed distraction. She needed something, anything to drown out the storm inside her chest.

Sleep had been a stranger. All through the night, she'd tossed and turned, her thoughts tangled in the bitter words exchanged with Hendry. Each syllable he'd spoken had landed like a blade. Clean cutting and impossibly precise. He had not shouted. Not raged. But, oh, how it had hurt.

And worse... he'd been *right*.

She stood now beside her sister's family, half-listening to the whispered prayers, and the murmurs of the gathered crowd. But her mind was far away, replaying again the fury in Hendry's eyes, the crack in his voice when he'd asked why she hadn't waited.

How had it come to this?

What she and Hendry had was rare, a true love. But she'd been so foolish. The moment Brant whispered doubt into her ear, wrapped it in calm logic and gentle hands, she'd let it burrow in. She hadn't questioned him. Hadn't fought against his words. Instead, she'd clung to the searing pain of her broken heart and convinced herself that Hendry had betrayed her in every way that mattered.

And it had all been lies.

Brant had been clever, too clever. He hadn't stormed in with accusations. No, he'd been patient. Gentle. He'd soothed her tears and offered comfort when Hendry's absence grew long.

She saw it all now, in agonizing clarity. Brant had spun his lies carefully. Like a spider luring prey into a web she hadn't even realized she'd walked into.

Her sister had known. Erin had warned her, tearfully begging her to wait. To give Hendry the chance to explain when he returned. But Ailith had refused. Blinded by grief and fear, she'd hardened her heart and rushed into a marriage meant to heal the wound Hendry left behind. Instead, it had deepened it.

Their marriage had been a prison of silence and suspicion. Slowly, subtly, he'd isolated her. Urged her to stay near the cottage. Offered to run her errands. Encouraged her to rest, to trust him. And in doing so, he'd kept her from the village, from the other warriors. From the truth.

Brant had driven a wedge between her and her family. Erin's visits had grown less frequent. Each one more uncomfortable than the last, until finally they stopped altogether. Ailith remembered those afternoons, when she and Erin sat down to talk, how Brant would sit in his chair like a warden. Arms crossed, eyes narrowed, saying little but hearing everything. No warmth. No joy. Just cold possession.

And through it all, she had defended him. Made excuses. Convinced herself that this was her life now, and she would bear it as women must, without complaint.

But standing here now, watching the gallows rise, a grim structure against the grey sky, Ailith couldn't lie to herself anymore.

She had wronged Hendry.

She had condemned him in her heart without proof, without question, and now… she'd lost him forever.

Her throat tightened. Her eyes burned with tears of shame.

And the unbearable truth that she would never have the chance to make it right.

"Look," Erin whispered, breaking Ailith from the swirl of regret and memory. "The guard has arrived."

The thunder of hooves preceded them. Twelve mounted warriors riding two by two into the village square, their warhorses immense, their breath misting the cold morning air. The ground trembled beneath their weight, each hoof falling like a warning. The crowd instinctively parted, forming a narrow corridor.

The guards came first, their chainmail catching what little light bled from the grey sky. Then came the prisoners.

Three men.

Each sat atop a horse, flanked by a warrior. Shackled. Broken.

Two hung their heads, shoulders slumped in resignation, their very postures weighted with defeat. The third was unraveling before their eyes, sobbing openly, his tear-streaked face scanning the crowd with unhinged desperation.

"Help me!" he cried, his voice cracking with desperation. "Please, someone, help!"

Ailith turned away.

She couldn't bear it. She couldn't allow pity to crack through. These men had committed terrible crimes. Had beaten and killed innocent people without mercy. How dare that one ask for help. For the one thing he denied those who were left dying or dead in his wake.

Her gaze drifted, searching for a safer anchor. And then she found him.

Two more horsemen approached at a slower, deliberate pace. One was Laird Alexander Ross, regal and unyielding. His very presence cloaked in the authority of his station. But it was the man beside him who stole her breath.

Hendry.

He looked every inch the warrior he'd always been, broad-shouldered, battle-hardened, silent. But something was different now. The way he sat his horse, so still, so composed, like a beautiful statue. Almost as if he was hollow inside.

His face was unreadable. No anger. No satisfaction. Then she noticed it, he was devoid of emotion. The hard line of his jaw and the dead calm in his eyes were the epitome of a hardened warrior.

When the laird and Hendry reached the front, both men reined in their mounts and turned to face the gathered crowd. Behind them, the prisoners were yanked from their horses like sacks of grain. The laird's warriors moved with brutal efficiency, dragging the condemned toward the gallows. Their struggles pathetic against men trained for war.

Ailith flinched as one of the prisoners was hauled up by the arms, his feet scraping against the wooden steps of the platform. The air grew heavier with every moment, the hush spreading like a blanket over the villagers.

Laird Ross raised a hand, and the murmurs stilled.

"Today," he said, voice carrying over the heads of the crowd, "justice will be served."

Ailith felt her sister tense beside her.

"These men," the laird continued, "attacked the innocent. Defenseless. They killed without mercy, and now they will receive none in return."

A wave of murmured approval swept through the crowd like a breeze, though it was tinged with sorrow, not triumph. Some cheered. Others cried.

The laird lifted his hand again. Silence returned like a breath held tight.

"The punishment will be named by my warrior, Hendry McNichol, who was left for dead by these very men."

The prisoners turned in unison, three broken faces staring at the man who now held their fate. But Hendry didn't meet their eyes.

He sat motionless, as if carved from stone.

No flicker of emotion crossed his face. No sign of hesitation.

"Death by hanging," Hendry called out, in a deep flat tone.

A ripple of sound followed, cries of relief, of grief, of anguish. Some wept for the lives lost. Others, perhaps, for the ones about to be hung.

The nooses were lowered. The man who had cried out

moments earlier sagged, his legs giving way. Whether from fear or unconsciousness, Ailith couldn't tell.

She looked away.

She couldn't watch death unfold, even if it was deserved. She had seen enough sorrow. Enough pain. Her heart was already fraying at the edges.

Beside her, Erin let out a soft gasp. In her arms, the bairn cooed. A gurgling sound that didn't belong in a place like this, so pure, so unaffected by the violence of the world.

Ailith reached over and gently touched the child's cheek, soft and dewy with the cold. The baby blinked up at her and then curled its tiny fingers around hers.

Ailith smiled, though it trembled on her lips. In the shadow of gallows and grief, life clung fiercely to the edges.

AILITH AND ERIN made their way toward her sister's home. Ailith took the bairn so that Erin could duck into the bakery to purchase bread for their last meal. Teller trailed behind, in hopes of getting scraps of fresh bread.

The dog exited first, a hunk of crusty bread in his mouth.

"Elias is always so kind to ye," she said to the dog, who chewed the treat.

She looked to the village square where the gallows still loomed.

After lingering to watch the now dead men being lowered and placed on the back of wagons, the crowd had begun to drift away in slow waves, some subdued, others weeping.

Ailith stood unmoving, her gaze fixed on the earth beneath

her boots.

"Ailith?" Erin asked gently, reaching to touch her arm. "What is the matter?"

Ailith didn't answer at first. She swallowed hard, eyes misting. Then she lifted her head and looked at her sister, her voice hoarse from everything she hadn't said.

"I should have listened to ye."

Erin blinked, brows rising. "What do ye mean?"

Ailith let out a shaky breath, brushing wind-tangled hair back from her face. "Back then… when Brant came to me with his lies and his false concern. When he told me Hendry had betrayed me, that he he'd lain with women the entire time of our relationship and I believed him. I let the shock and grief blind me. And ye…ye told me to wait. To speak with Hendry when he returned. But I didn't."

Erin's expression softened, her eyes already glistening. "Ailith…"

"I married Brant not out of love," Ailith pressed on, her voice cracking. "But out of hurt. I wanted to erase Hendry. I wanted to prove that I didn't need him. That I could move on. But I couldn't. Not really."

She let out a shaky breath, twisting the hem of her cloak in her hands.

"He came to my cottage yesterday. We spoke." Her lips trembled.

Erin placed a hand on her arm, steadying her.

"He was furious, but it wasn't his rage that cut me; it was his disappointment. His heartbreak. And it was justified. I believed the worst of him. Without ever giving him the benefit of a doubt."

"Ye were hurting," Erin said softly. "Ye loved each other fiercely. That kind of love, it can turn to fire if it's wounded."

Ailith nodded, eyes burning. "I see it in his face today. He's changed. There was a hollowness in him I'd never seen before. And I wonder if I was the one who carved it into him."

Erin's grip on her arm tightened slightly. "What did he say?"

Ailith wiped at her cheek with the edge of her sleeve. "That I didn't give him the chance to explain. That I believed a lie without fighting for him. And he's right. That is what I did."

A heavy silence settled between them, filled only by the quiet gurgles of the bairn, whose presence felt like a tether to something good.

"It is finally done," Ailith whispered, voice breaking. "He will never trust me again. And rightly so."

Erin took her hand, gave it a squeeze. "Ailith. Will ye fight for him?"

"I-I cannae, there is nothing left to be said. We can never recover from th-this," Ailith stuttered. "It is best if I move forward and not look back."

"The Ailith I ken does nae give up so easily," Erin pressed on. "My strong sister is a survivor, a fighter. He is yer one and only Ailith, why will ye nae fight for him? Show him how ye truly feel."

A realization hit her that she had to make things right. Had to show Hendry that she loved him more than anything in her life. Even if he never forgave her, she would seek him out and do her best to ensure he understood how sorry she was. Yes. She would fight for him. Fight so that joy returned to his eyes. So that he could continue on, to live life again without the burden of her betrayal.

She looked toward the path where Hendry had disappeared after the execution.

"I'll fight for him this time. Even if he doesn't want me to."

That night, sleeping on the floor of her sister's humble home, with Teller at her side, Ailith tried to formulate a plan. A way to do right by Hendry. But exhaustion from lack of sleep and the happenings of the day dragged her into a deep slumber.

*Five days later*

DESPITE THE BITTER wind that nipped at her cheeks and tugged at the hem of her cloak, the sun shone with unexpected brilliance. Its golden light spilling across the frost-kissed earth. Ailith stepped into the morning, a basket of feed in hand and a soft resolve settling deeper in her chest.

It was two days after the executions.

A day when death still lingered in the minds of the villagers, but for Ailith, it marked something else. A beginning.

Her path to healing had to start somewhere, and oddly enough, it began with the grumpy gray donkey now blinking at her from the gate.

The creature, stubborn and shaggy, had been her first investment since the storm that had torn her heart wide open. She'd used a portion of the coin Hendry had sent her, money she'd ignored out of pride, and purchased the donkey and a newly crafted cart from a local man, Erin's husband had vouched for. It had felt strange, freeing even, to finally buy something without fear of having to sell it back.

She'd gone to the sale with her brother-in-law by her side, his easy haggling and sharp eye ensuring she got a fair price. For once, she hadn't felt like someone being rescued, but like someone reclaiming her place in the world.

Now the donkey snorted as she approached, tail flicking lazily. Teller bounded around in excited circles, clearly believing the new addition was meant to be his personal playmate.

"Ye'll scare the poor beast half to madness," she said with a quiet laugh, pulling a carrot from her apron pocket.

The donkey took it with measured dignity, chewing slowly while giving Teller a side-eye of supreme disinterest.

"Told ye," Ailith murmured as she laid a thick blanket over the donkey's back. "Not everything wants to chase ye through the fields."

Once the animal had drunk its fill and inspected every corner of the trough with great solemnity, she led it to the small shelter near the edge of her property. The same pen where her old donkey had once dozed through long winters. She latched the gate, watching the animal nudge the straw as it settled in.

Inside, the cottage was quiet, warm with the scent of dried herbs and the faint crackle of the fire. She gathered her embroidery from the table, a half-finished floral pattern she'd been commissioned to stitch into a set of handkerchiefs. Since her last visit to the village market, orders had tripled. If she kept up the pace, she'd have enough to see her comfortably through the winter and perhaps even spring.

It wasn't wealth.

But it was hers.

A scratching at the door drew her gaze. She opened it and raised a brow. Teller sat there, tail wagging, ears perked with exaggerated innocence. "The donkey still wants nothing to do with ye."

The dog gave her a long-suffering stare, the kind that somehow managed to look both accusing and expectant.

"Oh, very well," she sighed, smiling. "A treat for yer trouble."

She retrieved the meaty bone she'd saved on the windowsill to keep cool and handed it over to the now triumphant hound. Teller retreated to his favorite place in front of the hearth, tail wagging furiously as he gnawed contentedly.

Ailith returned to her chair, needle in hand, cloth stretched between her fingers, but her thoughts didn't rest on thread or patterns. They drifted back to Hendry.

To his silence. To the hardness in his eyes. To the way he'd pronounced judgment like a man no longer tethered to the world. Her needle paused mid-stitch.

Could she reach him now? After all that had been said.

She didn't know.

But the thought of doing nothing, of letting that distance calcify into something permanent, was unbearable.

Ailith glanced out the window to the sun, still shining stubbornly despite the cold.

# CHAPTER TEN

By mid-afternoon, the wind had risen to a persistent howl, tugging at the shutters on Hendry's cottage like a restless spirit demanding entry. The wooden slats rattled with each gust, but he paid them no mind. Inside, all was quiet, save for the slow, methodical rasp of steel against stone.

Hendry sat hunched at his small table, the familiar weight of a dagger in one hand, a whetstone in the other. He didn't need it sharpened. It was already honed to perfection. But the motion, the scrape and drag, offered the rhythm and noise he required.

Sword training had ended. First meal had long since passed. The keep had emptied out, each warrior tending to his duties. The day slipping into the quiet lull that followed the morning rush.

Hendry, not scheduled for patrol until the next morning, had filled every hour with distraction. He'd brushed down his horse until its coat gleamed. Cleaned every corner of his cottage until even the hearthstones shone. Then gathering his soiled clothing, he had trudged to the laundry.

The laundress had stared at him as if he'd grown a second head, trying to snatch the bundle from his hands with a scolding mutter. He'd let her take it, eventually, but not before scrubbing the first tunic himself, just to fill the time.

All of it was a futile effort to drown his own thoughts. Of the look of sheer shock when he'd last spoken to Ailith.

The scrape of blade on stone faltered as a knock echoed against the door.

He didn't look up.

"If it's Tobin," he called gruffly, "I'm not hungry. And I dinnae care if the stable roof's fallen in."

The door creaked open anyway.

Hendry glanced up with a frown to find one of the stable hands, barely more than a lad with hair sticking out in every direction, wringing the edge of his tunic.

"S-sorry, sir," the boy stammered. "Didnae mean to interrupt. I was told to bring this to ye." He held out a basket.

Hendry didn't reach for it. Instead, he pointed to the table with the edge of his blade. "Who gave it to ye?"

The boy nearly tripped over his feet as he rushed forward, setting the basket down with an unceremonious thump. A linen cloth, embroidered with vines and tiny blossoms, covered the contents.

"A woman," he muttered. "Dunna ken her name." And with a quick nod, he fled, closing the door behind him with a sharp thud.

Hendry set the whetstone aside. His fingers, steady moments before, now trembled slightly as he reached for the basket.

It wasn't from his mother. She would have come herself, rapped at the door, and walked right in with arms spread for a hug. Her keen eyes taking him in for any sign of injury or thinness from skipped meals.

This... this was different.

Carefully, he lifted the embroidered cloth.

The scent struck him first, sweetness and spices.

*Baked apples.*

He stared down at the two half-moon pastries tucked into the linen, their crimped edges golden from sugar caramelized at the seams. His breath hitched. They were folded pies, his favorite. Something Ailith used to make when the trees were heavy with fruit, and the days had grown short.

He forced himself to open the second bundle.

Roasted chestnuts.

His throat tightened.

Before even reaching for the jug, he knew what it was. He uncorked it, brought it to his nose, and breathed in the rich scent of honeyed wine. She'd always made it for him in the colder months, knowing how he preferred it warm and spiced.

All of it. Every item in the basket had been made with him in mind. The food and drink he loved. The ones she remembered. The ones no one else would ken.

His body tightened as he stared down at the offering. Was she trying to undo what years of heartbreak had done with this?

Instead of soothing his troubled soul, the offerings made Hendry angry. The silence of the room seemed to press in tighter. The food sat there, fragrant, a message without words. Ailith was trying to make amends.

That she had believed a near stranger, not giving him the benefit of the doubt, waiting for him to return. No. Instead she'd quickly married the lying man leaving Hendry to wonder what had occurred.

A pang in his chest brought back a rush of emotions. The

physical pain he'd felt at returning to find his woman married to another. Having to hide from everyone to cry in private as his entire body shuddered with tears pouring down his face.

He'd vowed never to allow himself to love again. To not leave himself open to betrayal.

The wind rattled the shutters, and he stood to ensure they remained latched. A question entered his mind. Had Ailith brought the basket to the keep?

The thought stopped him cold.

He swallowed hard. His gaze flicking to the window. Had she sent the basket and fled? Or… was she still there at the keep?

With a grunt, he returned to the table, picked up a dagger, and began to sharpen it. He would not give in. No matter how much he still loved Ailith, he had to remember that she had the power to destroy him.

JUST BEFORE LAST meal, Hendry, Liam, and Cynden stood before their men. Each leader took a turn asking for reports, giving orders, and praising when it was warranted. Then the men were released. Those who lived elsewhere headed home, and those who lived there returned to their quarters or to the great room to await last meal.

Many of the warriors adjured to the kitchen area within the guard's quarters. In the small space where an archer, called Joshua, sometimes cooked for the group. Hendry had eaten there a few times and had been impressed.

It was often said that Joshua's cooking rivaled that of the keep's cook, which made for a friendly competition.

Hendry glanced to the keep and then toward the guard's

quarters. If Joshua cooked, it would be only enough for about six men, so he decided he wouldn't go there and take from their portions. For a moment, he considered skipping last meal, but he was already hungry and by the time he began patrolling the following morning, he'd be too hungry to properly focus.

"Ye looked undecided," Liam said with a lopsided grin. Then sniffing the air he added, "It smells like roasted hog."

Indeed the smoky aroma made Hendry's stomach rumble. "I am very hungry."

Together they walked to the main entrance, into the wide foyer, and turned left into the great room.

Already servants meandered about with trays laden with baskets of bread, platters heaped high with sliced roast pork, and bowls filled with fragrant steamed potatoes. Others carried pitchers, one in each hand pouring and refilling tankards as they went. An older harried woman hurried to Hendry and glanced up at him. "Sir, the laird wishes a word with ye."

Hendry nodded at the woman who turned and rushed toward the kitchens.

"What do ye think it is about?" Liam asked having overheard what the woman had said.

Scanning the room, he didn't see Ailith, so he shook his head. "Probably about the executions. We've nae had time to discuss it."

Hendry walked toward the high board, every so often looking to each table.

Just as he reached where Alexander sat, he saw her. Ailith. She sat with Nala, Alexander's wife, as well as Ainsley, Cynden's wife, at the table where the women who lived at the keep usually sat. It was a round table to the left of the high board. Except for when important visitors were expected, Lady Nala, preferred the company of women during last meal. Often citing she and Alexander didn't have privacy to discuss personal matters at the high board.

Upon reaching the high board, Alexander motioned to an empty seat on his left. "Sit. Eat with us."

Obviously, the seats had been saved for them. Often Alexander invited them to join him, since only one of his siblings, Cynden, still lived there.

He lowered to a chair and was immediately served by a maid who remained close in case the laird required anything. He thanked the young woman, who blushed prettily and moved to refill tankards.

"Did ye note that Ailith is here?" the laird asked. "She has requested an audience with me in the morning."

Hendry looked toward Ailith, who kept her gaze down. "An audience. Did she state what about?"

"She did nae," Alexander said, meeting his gaze. "Do ye have any idea what it would be about?"

Spearing meat and biting into it, he almost moaned at how delicious the pork was. Hendry shook his head. "I spoke to her two days ago. Found out that Brant lied to get her to marry him. She was shaken at hearing the truth."

Hesitating, he glanced once again toward Ailith. "We also spoke on the subject of Brant's death and how she'd falsely accused the warriors that had fought alongside him to be at fault. When I explained the bond between the men, she was stricken."

Alexander's brow furrowed. "She refused the widow's

allowance and has struggled to survive because of pride."

It was astounding how much Alexander knew about the clans' people. Laird Ross was a man who cared for his people, who fought for them, and would not allow any suffering that could be avoided. It made sense that he was informed about Ailith.

"I ken. In return for her helping me when I was injured, I sent food, blankets, and coin. Surprisingly, she accepted the recompense."

Both men were silent. "That is very surprising," Alexander murmured. "I ken ye were in a bad way after she married Brant. How do ye feel about her now?"

"It matters not," Hendry replied, carefully stacking meat and a chunk of potato, anticipating the bite. Chewing on the morsel, he looked toward the entrance, willing someone to enter with news. Any news. A fight in the pub. A horse loose in the village square. An archer with an arrow through his head. He wasn't picky. Anything to get Alexander to change the subject.

The great hall fell into sudden silence the moment two warriors burst through the doors, their cloaks tattered, boots caked in mud, and chests heaving for breath. They looked as if they'd ridden through a storm.

Hendry's eyes locked on them, widening. It was as if his very thoughts had summoned them.

No blood. No visible wounds. Thank the saints.

Tankards halted midair. Conversations died mid-sentence. Every gaze in the room snapped toward the warriors as they strode across the stone floor, their boots and armor the only sounds.

"A word, Laird. 'Tis urgent," one of them said, glancing between Alexander and Hendry, his face pale with tension. "In private, sire."

Without hesitation, Cynden, Liam, and Hendry stood and followed the laird and the two warriors through a side door. The wooden panel slamming shut behind them. The chill outside bit instantly, but it was the warriors' next words that truly froze the air.

"Birlinns, coming from the south. Bearing MacLeod banners."

Alexander let out a low curse. "Again? We must prepare to defend, in case it is trouble they are after." He turned sharply to the three leaders. "Deploy yer men. Now."

Hendry didn't answer. He was already running. Liam and Cynden alongside.

His boots seemed to fly over the packed courtyard ground as he sprinted toward the guard quarters, barking orders as he went. "To arms! Dress for battle! Mount up!"

The courtyard exploded into organized chaos.

Men scrambled into action, racing to the armory. Once there jerking on leather and mail. Scabbards were thrown over wide backs. Swords and claymores gleamed in the growing light. Short swords were slid into hip holsters and daggers tucked into straps across broad chests. Within moments, every man was fully armed for battle.

Liam's orders were carried to Hendry as he rallied the archers. Squires darted among huge war horses, arms laden with quivers, tossing them to the archers who stood at the ready, bowstrings already taut. Cynden did the same. His men, a combination of guards and archers, manning the top of the wall surrounding the keep.

War cries filled the air as warriors prepared for blood. Horses were led out, stamping and snorting, sensing the coming storm. Liam and Hendry mounted, their cloaks snapping like banners behind them as they rode out of the wide keep gates. Scouts rode ahead. Flank riders moved into position. Then, letting out war cries the Ross army thundered from the keep like a living beast set loose.

Hendry rode hard, his thoughts flashing back, Brant, fallen in the last clash with the MacLeods. And now Ailith was back within the keep's walls while the same threat stirred once more.

As they crested the southern ridge, the coastline came into view. Ross birlinns were already gliding from the shore, oars slicing the water in synchronized rhythm. The first line of defense surged forward to intercept the threat.

Archers stood at the prow, bows drawn. Behind them, warriors bristling with crossbows and battle axes waited for the order to strike.

Even in the face of battle, Hendry felt it, that tight burn in his chest. Not fear. Not dread.

Pride. Fierce and unshakable.

# CHAPTER ELEVEN

"I'll find out what's happening." Nala, the laird's wife, rose swiftly, her skirts swaying side to side as she made her way toward the entrance.

The laird walked toward the high board, his stride purposeful and eyes grave. Without hesitation, Nala met him and slipped her hand into the crook of his arm. He stopped and leaned in, his lips brushing close to her ear, sharing a message meant only for her.

Ailith's heart clenched. The sight of them, united, steady, and still so openly in love, stirred a pain deep within her. They moved as one, partners in every way, offering strength and compassion to their people with a single glance exchanged between them.

The stern laird a hardened warrior seemed to soften at his wife's nearness, his strong body a sharp contrast to the soft curves of his wife, who was a trained swordswoman and rumored to be a fierce fighter. And yet each time they spoke to each other, it was as if they were one.

It was a love Ailith had once known. And lost.

"They're headed to the high board," Ainslie whispered beside her, not taking her eyes off the couple. "Alexander's going to make an announcement."

A chill coiled around Ailith's spine. Dread whispered its

warning in the back of her mind. Whatever news the laird carried, it would not be good. She'd seen the three leaders, Liam, Cynden, and Hendry, and all the warriors rush from the room.

Now, silence gripped the space like a vice. Conversations had died. Even the smallest sounds, the creak of benches, the rustle of skirts, seemed too loud. The tension crackled in the air, thick and tangible.

Ailith didn't dare breathe as the laird stepped forward, his tall frame commanding attention, his gaze sweeping across every face.

"Clan MacLeod," he began, his voice clear and steady, "has been seen approaching from the south, by sea. My army has ridden out to meet them. The keep's defenses have been fortified. Ye are safe here."

He paused, his tone softening as he drew his wife nearer, their silhouettes a portrait of strength and devotion. "Remain calm. No one is to leave the hall until we've ensured the threat has passed. Supplies will be brought in. Blankets, food, anything needed."

Then, solemnly, he added, "Pray for our warriors. They are fierce and well-prepared, and they fight not just with steel, but with the fire of loyalty to this clan. I have every faith they will return victorious."

The room remained hushed, but it felt different now, heavier. Ailith's vision swam, the edges of her world blurring. Her heart pounded painfully in her chest, too loud in the silence. Thank the heavens she was seated. Her legs trembled beneath her like reeds in a storm. The fear she'd tried to hold back was no longer a whisper. It was roaring in her veins.

In the waning sun… Hendry was riding toward danger.

"Come there is much to do," Nala called out as she walked past their table, motioning to her and Ainslie to follow. Several other women joined the procession behind Nala, some having to run in order to keep up.

Hesitating just as they exited the great room, Nala turned and scanned the women assembled. "Emma, Nellie, and Ingrid, go with the chambermaids to fetch extra blankets." She divided the women into teams, sending some to the well for water, others to help in the kitchen, and another group to fetch straw for bedding.

Ailith went with two others to the laundry to help with the washing of any bedding and hanging the items out to dry.

The laundry was a spacious room with lines of clay and rock basins with slanted lips used for scrubbing. A huge pot with steam emanating from it was being stirred, the smell of lye strong in the air.

The laundress was a tall woman with a more masculine than feminine frame. With a kerchief tied atop her head to keep hair out of her face, she barely glanced at them when they entered.

"There are sheets on the lines that need to be gathered," she said, pointing to one of Ailith's companions. "Go fetch them, fold them, and put them on the table just outside the door with the others."

Her sharp gaze took Ailith in, then slid down to where Teller stood next to her. Her faithful dog, who'd been sleeping under the table, had followed her. "Take that stack of clothes there to the warrior, Beathan's, cottage. Return to help collect extra bedding."

She told the woman standing with Ailith much the same thing; the only difference was to take her bundles to a different warrior's cottage. Upon walking out, Ailith looked to the other woman. "Do ye work here?"

"Aye, I work serving the laird."

"I can take these to the cottages," she said. Just tell me where to go.

The woman shrugged. "Fine. Beathan's is there," she pointed to a cottage near the stables. "Hendry's is further, along the back wall." Again she pointed. "Thank ye I have to return to ensure the laird is not in need of anything."

She took the bundle, and the woman hurried away. There were three cottages along the back wall of the keep. Ailith called for Teller, who'd gone a short distance away, sniffing everything, excited at all the new smells.

A stable lad had been more than enthusiastic, giving her more directions than were necessary when the trio of cottages were clearly visible from where they stood. Hendry's cottage was on the end, the furthest from the keep.

For some reason she knocked before pushing the door open. "Is anyone here?" she called out just to be sure.

"Stay here," she ordered Teller, who lowered his haunches in obedience.

Then she walked in.

The space was simple... and spotless. The floors were swept, the hearth cleaned, and every surface looked to have been scrubbed. A bed was on the left, under it a braided rug. There was a trunk at the foot, where she assumed he kept his clothes.

Next to the bed was a three-legged table, upon which was a lantern, nothing more. On the right there was a hearth, the fire doused. Next to it a tall slender table with a shelf underneath. There were several cups, a bowl, and a small iron pot for boiling water.

In the center of the room was a table with three chairs. Her eyes focused on the small basket in the center. It was the one she'd sent to him upon arriving that morning.

First, she placed the neatly folded clothes atop the trunk, not wishing to overstep by opening it.

Moving slowly, not quite sure what to expect, she went to the table. The cloth had been folded over the items inside. Lifting one corner, she peered in and let out a breath.

The sack of roasted chestnuts was gone and one of the pies was no longer there. He'd eaten the pie. The knowledge made her breathe easier.

It was a small step. Hopefully, it meant he would come to forgive her in time.

When she made it to the door, she turned to look at the room and took in every detail. This was the place the man she'd once planned to marry lived. How different their lives had turned out.

Ailith closed her eyes. This was not the time for sentimentalities. Her energy would go toward helping in any way she could and praying for Hendry's safe return.

# CHAPTER TWELVE

THE SUN BLED into the horizon, casting a fiery glow that did little to warm the creeping chill in the air. Dusk approached swiftly, and with it came the unnerving awareness of the situation at hand. The timing was no accident. The MacLeod birlinns had arrived late, their long, shadowed vessels slicing through the darkening sea like silent blades. They wanted nightfall. Darkness favored chaos.

Along the shoreline, giant bonfires roared to life. Their flames clawing at the sky. Their flickering light illuminated the rocky coastline, casting shadows over the figures gathered below. The Ross army had begun to settle in for a cold, merciless night that would test the strength of both body and spirit. The fires were not just for warmth, but to help them maintain a vigil all night, if needed.

On the ridge, Hendry stood with some of his men. The cloak across his shoulders, falling to below his knees. His eyes scanned the open water, jaw clenched tight. To either side of them, archers held their bows half-drawn. Their muscles taut as bowstrings, ready to loose death at the first sign of a clash.

Below, Ross warriors moved in restless circles along the shoreline, reminding one of silent predators. Wolves pacing the edge of a hunt. Their expressions were grim, the firelight flickering across determined faces. Every eye was fixed on the sea where the enemy hovered, a maddeningly still threat.

The MacLeod birlinns lingered just beyond reach, their sails furled, their warriors obscured by distance and dusk. They floated like specters. Waiting. Watching. The Ross boats had yet to reach them, carrying warriors under command to keep their weapons at the ready. Cynden was among them, his form indistinct. He was there to negotiate. To attempt to broker a fragile peace in his brother's name.

But Hendry's gut twisted.

There was no trust to be had with MacLeods. Their warriors were bred on vengeance and violence, known to butcher opponents without mercy. They cared nothing for honor, nor for pity. And the most dangerous enemy, Hendry knew, was one who didnae fear death, who charged into battle not to survive, but to destroy.

The wind shifted, and a sudden gust blew smoke from the bonfires up toward the cliffs. Hendry inhaled it like a war omen. The waiting would soon end, bringing with it war or peace.

A horn sounded.

Not from the sea, but from inland.

The blast echoed off the cliffs like a scream, sharp and sudden, slicing through the sounds of battle and the sea's crashing waves. Hendry's head snapped toward the hills behind them, his heart thundering in his ears. His gut instinct firing off warnings, which must have been the same for the other Ross warriors because at the sound, the archers split, every other one turning from the sea to the land.

Shouts rose from below, warriors turning away from the water, confused, uncertain whether the sound was friend or foe. Then came the answer. Again being experienced, half remained focused on those out to sea, whilst the rest turned and headed up the hill.

Another horn. Then a third.

"From the east!" several of the archers yelled, pointing toward the tree line. "MacLeods!"

From the shadows of the dense forest, shapes surged forward. Scores of MacLeod warriors burst forth, battle-maddened and roaring like demons loosed from hell. They poured over the rocky rise, axes raised, blades glinting in the firelight. Their war cries were unhinged, guttural. The sound didn't intimidate the Ross army; instead, it seemed to invigorate them as they returned with battle cries of their own.

"Shields up!" Hendry bellowed, his voice cutting across the clamor. "To me! Form ranks! Protect the archers!"

The Ross men obeyed without hesitation, instinct and training taking hold. Swords hissed free, shields locked, and the line braced just as the MacLeods slammed into them with bone-jarring force.

The clash was deafening. Steel upon steel. The sickening crunch of blade meeting bone. Hendry ducked a wild swing and drove his sword into the attacker's ribs, wrenching it free as another charged from the side. Blood sprayed. The metallic odor sharp in the air.

From the shoreline, the Ross warriors surged up the incline to join the fray, abandoning the sea and their watch. Just as a second eruption of chaos shattered the horizon.

Moving backward to see if more warriors were needed, Hendry caught sight of Ross warriors boarding more birlinns to head out and help.

A roar went up from the birlinns on the water. Shouts, clashing steel, and the entangled bodies of men fighting and falling overboard. There had been no negotiations. It had all been a ploy, a coordinated ambush by land and sea.

Steel clanged against wood.

Oars snapped.

The men fought atop slick decks, the cold spray of seawater mixing with the red of fresh wounds. A Ross warrior was thrown overboard, arms flailing, before the dark water swallowed him whole. Cynden, blood streaking his cheek, fought like a man possessed. blade carving a path through the chaos as the Ross men rallied to protect their commander.

Hendry's stomach dropped. "They're attacking everywhere," he muttered, rage and dread knotting in his chest. "Bastards planned the whole of it."

The Ross were under siege from two fronts, their warriors split, their defenses strained. The MacLeods had come not to test their strength, but to conquer.

Still, the Ross warriors held the line, their fury rising with every heartbeat. And if the MacLeods wanted blood, the Ross clan would drown them in it.

The night wore on, and with it came blood, sweat, and the unrelenting clang of steel.

The shoreline was a battlefield bathed in firelight. Smoke curled into the night sky, stinging eyes and coating lungs, while the screams of the wounded and the clash of swords rang out over the crashing waves.

Both sides had suffered many losses. The ground was slick with blood, the scent of iron thick and nauseating. Still, neither army gave way.

The Ross warriors fought with the discipline of hardened soldiers. The MacLeods, with the madness of men who had nothing left to lose.

"Fer Laird Calum!" one of the MacLeod men shouted, his face streaked with blood, a jagged wound slicing across his scalp. "Revenge for our fallen chief!"

The cry rippled through the MacLeod line like wildfire, igniting a second wind. They surged forward with renewed ferocity, teeth bared, eyes wild.

Hendry gritted his teeth and raised his shield just in time to deflect a blow that would have split his skull. He countered with a swift strike, cutting deep into the man's thigh and dropping him with a scream.

"They'll nae stop," a Ross warrior growled beside him, panting. "They'll die before they retreat."

"Aye," Hendry called back, his chest heaving. "Then we'll make certain they do."

The fighting dragged on, and even the fiercest blades began to slow.

Muscles burned.

Vision blurred.

Men slipped in the mud and blood, rising only to fall again beneath another's sword. Exhaustion clawed at every limb, but retreat wasn't an option. To fall back now meant losing the keep. The village. Their families.

And still, the MacLeods kept fighting.

Sometime during the battle, Alexander and a group from the keep had joined in the fray. Their presence renewing them, but it didn't last long.

Hendry's arms ached with each swing. His legs felt like

stone. Beside him, a warrior crumpled to the ground, a blade buried in his back. Hendry didn't have time to mourn; he had to live long enough to protect the others. His blade met another, sparks flying as they locked. He twisted, drove his elbow into the enemy's face, then drove his blade deep into the man's chest.

He was turning to engage the next threat when a sound split the chaos. A horn. But not from the MacLeods.

It came from the west.

For a moment, no one moved. Heads turned. The MacLeods faltered, just for a breath, uncertainty flickering in their bloodshot eyes.

Then, through the haze and smoke, mounted warriors crested the hill, torches in hand, steel glinting beneath the moon. They came thundering down like a tide, war cries splitting the night.

"Ross! Ross! Ross!" The nearing warriors called out in unison, repeating the word over and over to ensure they were heard.

A rider in dark green plaid led the charge, his sword raised high, black hair whipping in the wind.

"Munro Ross!" someone cried out in disbelief. "He's come!" It was Alexander's brother who was laird of the southwestern portion of Skye.

The Ross warriors on the battlefield answered with a roar, their spirits reignited. Some wept, others laughed. Mad and breathless from relief, every man gripped his weapon tighter. Suddenly their strength renewed with hope.

Several of the arriving warriors had obviously been ordered by the laird's brother to surround and remove the laird because they circled Alexander, guiding the angry man out of the battlefield.

The MacLeods, caught between two forces now, began to falter. Some turned, only to be met by the new wave of Ross steel crashing into their flank.

Munro's men hit hard and fast, breaking the MacLeod line like a hammer through glass.

Hendry stumbled back from the fight just long enough to breathe. His vision found Munro, still on horseback, fighting like a man possessed. Their eyes met across the field, and Hendry gave a single, grateful nod.

The tide had turned.

It wasn't long before the battle was over.

What remained was silence, broken only by the moans of the wounded and the distant crash of waves upon the shore.

Bodies were strewn on the shoreline, on the hill, and in the clearing. Victory had been claimed, but it had not come without a cost.

Hendry stood amidst the carnage, his chest rising and falling in ragged breaths. His sword hung from his hand, slick with blood, its weight suddenly unbearable. Around him, Ross warriors moved like ghosts, checking the fallen, binding wounds, whispering names of the dead under their breath.

He turned toward the tree line where several MacLeod prisoners had been rounded up. Their weapons stripped. Their faces a mixture of defiance, shock, and grief. Among them, one stood apart, hands bound and surrounded by three Ross warriors with swords drawn and no tolerance for nonsense.

A grizzled man with a jagged scar across his cheek, shoulders squared despite the blood caked to his brow. His eyes, cold, gray, and far too calm for a man who had just lost a war, locked on Hendry.

"Who is he?" Hendry asked as he approached. He, too, was streaked with blood and smoke, his hair wind-tossed and his jaw clenched tight.

"Donnan MacLeod," Munro answered grimly. "Brother to the late Laird Calum. Likely the one who led the inland strike."

Hendry approached the man slowly, the firelight flickering over his face. "Ye led yer warriors into a trap," he said flatly. "One ye thought we'd be too blind to see."

Donnan let out a slow breath, a cruel smile curling his lips. "And yet, we nearly split yer forces. Nearly razed yer defenses." He turned his gaze to Hendry. "Tell me, did yer laird piss himself when he heard we were coming?"

Hendry didn't respond. He didn't need to.

Instead, he walked forward and backhanded Donnan across the mouth, not out of anger, but to silence the venom before it spread further. Blood smeared across the MacLeod's chin, but his expression didn't change.

"We will bury enough men tonight," Hendry said coldly. "So unless ye wish to join them, hold yer tongue."

"Ye'll not kill him," Munro said after a beat. "He'll be taken back to the keep. He'll answer to Alexander and the council."

"Ye think a trial will stop men like me?" Donnan sneered. "We were born for war. Ye can take my head, another MacLeod will rise. Our feud does nae end here."

"No," Munro agreed, his voice low and even, "but ye do."

Donnan spat at his feet but said nothing else.

The Ross warriors hauled him back toward the path leading to the keep. As they disappeared into the shadows, Hendry let out a long breath, feeling the ache of every blow, every loss, every soul left behind.

The fires still burned, but now they gave off a different light. Less warning. More vigil.

He turned his gaze skyward, the stars finally breaking through the smoke. They had won. But it hadn't felt like a triumph.

It had felt like survival.

And tomorrow... tomorrow there would be names to speak, families to console, and a keep to fortify once more.

But tonight, they would mourn the dead and remember why they fought.

## CHAPTER THIRTEEN

AT FIRST, THE wounded came in a slow trickle, bloodied, groaning, some carried between two warriors. Then the flood began.

Men poured into the great hall, which had been hastily cleared of benches and banners to serve as a makeshift infirmary. The sharp cries of pain and the moans of the injured rose to the high timbered ceiling as they were laid upon the tabletops.

The air was thick with the scent of blood, sweat, and herbs. An insufferable mix of life and death intermingling in one space.

In the corridors just outside, women worked with frantic purpose, their fingers raw from tearing linen into bandage strips. Kitchen servants pounded herbs into pastes, the grinding of pestles against stone a constant, desperate rhythm. At every hearth, water boiled furiously, steam rising in ghostly plumes as boys and gray-haired elders dashed back and forth with brimming buckets to cleanse wounds and soak cloths.

The healers and their apprentices moved swiftly from man to man, their faces drawn, their hands slick with blood. A smear of ash across the forehead marked those closest to death. Those who needed tending immediately.

Ailith hurried in, an armful of fresh bandages clutched to

her chest, just as a scream split the air. A warrior writhed on a table, his leg a twisted ruin of bone and torn flesh. The grim-faced healer barked without looking up, "Drop that. Hold him down, I've got to take the leg."

The man thrashed, lifting his head and crying out, "No! Dinnae! It can heal!"

Ailith's breath caught when she saw the injury, only a single tendon clung to the mangled lower limb. Her stomach twisted. No healing could save that. She moved quickly, placing a firm hand on the warrior's shoulder.

"It'll heal," she lied, her voice low as she accepted a cup of whiskey laced with herbs and pressed it to his lips. "Drink. It'll dull the pain."

He drank, but not enough. The poor man howled in pain as the tether between flesh and bone was severed. She didn't look away. She couldn't. He was someone she'd seen before, laughing in the courtyard, sparring in the yard, a man now reduced to raw agony.

The moment it was over, the healer ordered the wound to be bound and wrapped as they moved on. There was no time for rest, no time for grief. Ash-marked men lay scattered across the floor, and the healer barely spared a breath before pointing to the next.

Ailith followed, her apron blood-soaked, her fingers trembling. A man they went to was already dead, and the healer whispered a prayer as he closed the man's eyes. "Come," he said hoarsely, "we go on."

She paused just a heartbeat longer. The man who'd passed was old, older than any warrior should've been on that field. "Ye were brave," she whispered, brushing her bloodied knuckles against his brow.

Her body ached. Muscles throbbed. Hours had bled into one another, and still the wounded came. As dawn's pale light trickled through the windows, they reached the last few injured. The healer cleaned and bandaged a gash and nodded. "He'll live."

He accepted a cup of honeyed wine and a piece of bread from a weary servant, then looked to those around him, exhausted, blood-streaked, hollow-eyed. "Eat. Drink. We begin second rounds shortly."

Ailith slumped onto a stool for the first time in hours, the basket of healing supplies slipping from her grip.

The battle was over. But the fight to keep them alive had only just begun.

Ailith hadn't seen Hendry.

Not among the injured brought in. Not with the laird, who had returned from the battlefield flanked by his closest advisors, their faces gray with exhaustion and grief. She'd searched every face in the overcrowded great room. Her eyes scanning each man laid out on pallets and tables, bodies packed shoulder to shoulder. Every surface was occupied. Twenty-three, by her last count. And still, none of them was Hendry.

The dead had been taken elsewhere. Whispers passed through the corridors said they were laid in neat rows along the side of the manor, draped in linen and watched over until the guards could bear them to their kin. Ailith hadn't dared to look. Not yet.

He had to be alive. He had to be.

The thought of anything having happened to him crippled

her. Fear tightening her chest until she could barely breathe.

She would never recover if he were gone. Surely fate would not be so cruel. With or without her, Hendry deserved a long and happy life, to fall in love again, to live a full life.

Outside, the courtyard was chaos, organized, desperate chaos. People hurried in every direction, some carrying water, others food. Small fires blazed where women cooked aromatic stews in iron pots. A few had erected makeshift shelters, wooden frames hastily lashed together and thatched with straw. Smoke curled upward into the gray morning light as families huddled near the warmth, keeping the chill at bay as best they could.

Past the well, she caught sight of a cluster of long tables just outside the kitchens. Women worked there with red-streaked hands, binding wounds, setting dislocated limbs, sewing gashes closed. One woman stitched a soldier's arm, and though his jaw clenched with every pass of the needle, he remained silent. Brave or numb, Ailith couldn't tell.

And then, she saw him.

Hendry.

He sat shirtless at the edge of a bench, hunched to his right, his face pale and drawn. A healer stood beside him, gently pouring water into a long cut on his left shoulder. His eyes were squeezed shut, jaw tight with pain, but he made no sound. The muscle along his jaw twitched with each touch.

Ailith's breath caught.

The healer spoke without looking up. "It will have to be stitched closed."

"I'll do it," Ailith said, her voice soft but firm as she stepped forward.

She stood beside him, reaching for clean cloths and thread. The wound was angry and red, but thankfully not too deep.

At the sound of her voice, Hendry opened his eyes.

Their gazes met.

And her heart dropped.

There was no recognition. No warmth. No anger. Not even indifference. Just… emptiness.

It was like he looked at a stranger.

Her hands faltered, just for a moment. She'd imagined him angry with her, perhaps even resentful. She'd even dared to hope for forgiveness, for some soft echo of what once lingered between them. But this…this utter absence was worse than any fury.

It was final.

Her throat tightened as she forced herself continue cleaning the wound, her hands steady even as her heart cracked apart. She had finally done it, pushed him far enough that there was nothing left. No anger. No affection. No trace that she'd ever meant anything to him at all.

Just…disregard.

Complete and utter disregard.

Ailith worked swiftly, her hands practiced, though her heart trembled with every stitch she placed in Hendry's shoulder. She focused on the wound, not the silence that circled them, tangible in the air.

He never once looked at her.

Not during the stitching. Not when she awkwardly asked him to lift his arm to bind the bandage in place. His eyes stared ahead, vacant and unblinking, as if she weren't there at all. As if no one was.

When she finished, he rose without a word, tugged his tunic on over the dressing with a wince, and turned away. His steps were uneven, staggering slightly as he moved across the courtyard, headed toward the practice field like a man summoned by ghosts.

She hesitated, then followed. Something was wrong, more than the pain of his injury, more than exhaustion. There was something broken in him now, something splintered so deeply it showed in every faltering step.

He wasn't the only one.

Other warriors emerged from the shadows of the keep, drifting across the yard like sleepwalkers. No one spoke. No nods of greeting. Just grim faces and hollow eyes. One man dragged his foot behind him, limping so severely Ailith considered rushing to help him, but instinct told her not to. They didn't want sympathy. They didn't want to be touched.

Then she saw it.

Her breath caught, hands flying to her mouth to stifle the gasp.

The practice field was no longer a place for drills or sport.

It had become a graveyard.

Bodies lay upon the cold earth, each one shrouded in linen. Some were stained dark with blood, telling silent tales of where the blade had entered, where life had spilled away.

Ailith didn't count them. She couldn't. Even one was too many.

Just yesterday, these men had laughed and broken bread together. They'd tended horses, kissed their wives, lifted their children. Now they lay still and silent beneath the morning sky.

People were already there, each drawn toward a familiar form. Some knelt. Others pressed shaking hands against covered chests. A few broke down entirely.

Hendry moved among them, purposeful but unsteady, until he reached one lone body at the end of a row.

He dropped to his knees, then collapsed forward, pulling back the linen with trembling hands. He stared at the face beneath, a guttural sound escaping his throat. Then he lowered his head onto the man's chest, shoulders quaking with silent sobs.

It undid her.

Tears spilled freely down Ailith's cheeks, hot and blinding. Around the field, men mourned their fallen brothers in arms, not as warriors, but as family. These weren't just soldiers bound by loyalty. They were brothers. They'd stood side by side, shield to shield.

She thought of Brant, of the bitter accusations she'd hurled in her grief, how she'd called the men who returned selfish, uncaring. Now she wondered how many of them had wept over her husband, whispered the last words he'd heard and laid hands on his heart as it stilled.

"It's best we leave them their privacy," Ainslie said quietly, her eyes fixed on her own husband, who knelt with his hand clenched around a fallen comrade's shoulder, the other covering his face as if to hold in the grief.

Ailith nodded, turning back toward the keep, her feet heavy, her soul heavier. She wiped at her face with the edge of her apron, but it did little to hide the tears.

"It's all so senseless," she whispered, her voice breaking. "Why? Why would anyone do this? What good comes of all this death?"

Ainslie's reply was tired, resolute. "Because some men want more and more power. With failure comes the need for vengeance. And so it happens… again and again."

They walked in silence for a moment before she added, "It will take days, weeks, for the warriors to recover. Some never will. All we can do now is to be there, to listen when they're ready. To soothe when they'll allow it. And sometimes… to walk away and let them grieve in their own way."

She reached up to brush away her own tears. Then she exhaled and straightened her shoulders.

"Come Ailith. We have wounded to tend to."

# CHAPTER FOURTEEN

By the time the night came this particular day, Hendry was barely able to trudge to his cottage. Had it been two or three days since he last slept? It didn't matter, he was still upright, which was better than others.

While mourning the loss of their comrades, men whom they'd trained with, worked with, and lived with, they still had duties to perform.

They'd spent days bringing bodies along with horrible news to mothers, wives, and children. The laird's guards helped to dig graves, helpless against the wails of breaking hearts and devastation.

Villagers had come and helped to bury the dead MacLeods. Although some had managed to escape during the chaos of battle, those captured were executed. Their bodies joining those already lining the mass grave.

It was a dark time for Clan Ross, an occurrence that would linger for days to come as the injured began to heal physically, though there were some who'd never return to battle.

Once inside his cottage, Hendry stripped off all his dirty clothes and threw the offensive items into a corner. Then using water his squire had brought, he washed the lingering smells of death and blood from his body. A proper bath would have to wait. He was much too exhausted to make his way to the loch or wait his turn at the bathing area near the kitchens.

Still fully naked, he fell onto the bed, praying for a dreamless slumber.

RAPS ON THE door woke Hendry and he pushed up from his bed, groggy and unsure of how long he'd slept. The door opened and Tobin walked in followed by two lads, each carrying a bucket of water.

Without a word, the squire went back out and with the same lads, rolled in a wooden tub.

"Sir, the water is warm. I brought it from the kitchens upon noting there was nae a line for bathing."

Looking to the window, it seemed the sun was either rising or falling. "Is it morning?"

Tobin shook his head. "It is close to last meal. Ye slept the entire night and most of this day." The squire motioned to the tub and Hendry went to it as the young man poured in the water, giving the empty buckets to the lads who rushed out to refill them.

Once the water was delivered, Hendry instructed Tobin to give each lad a copper coin.

Sending his squire away, Hendry bathed with quick movements. Although his muscles ached, and the warm water helped to soothe them, he didn't have time to linger. Once cleansed, he would go to the great hall to eat and help wherever was needed.

Hendry had just fastened the ties of his breeches and was rummaging through his trunk for a tunic when a knock sounded at the door.

He paused, frowning. His squire never knocked. Neither

did the warriors under his command, they usually barged in, asking questions, and rarely cared for propriety.

"Enter," he called, returning to the tunic dilemma. Most were too worn, riddled with holes and stains. He finally settled on one that appeared mildly presentable, if still a bit threadbare.

"I brought ye something to eat."

He froze.

He didn't dare turn, afraid it was a trick of memory, or longing. But then her dog, Teller, trotted over and pawed gently at his leg, tail wagging and let out a cheerful bark.

"I'll set it on the table for ye," she continued. Her footsteps were soft but unsteady as she crossed the room, arms trembling under the weight of the tray she carried. She lowered it carefully onto the table, a hearty meal of roasted meat, a small pot of stew, and a basket of bread.

She clasped her hands in front of her, her eyes meeting his with a flicker of nervousness.

"Ye've not been to any meals," she said in a soft voice. "I asked yer squire, and he only said ye slept. He came just now to tell me ye were awake."

She looked utterly worn, her beautiful face drawn, dark shadows beneath her eyes hinting at sleepless nights. Still, she came. Still, she brought food.

He moved to the table and pulled out a chair. "Will ye join me?"

Ailith glanced at the hearth where Teller had curled up in front of the fire. With a tight smile, she lowered herself into the chair.

The silence between them wasn't strained, it was heavy,

yes, but familiar. The weight of shared grief. Shared battles. Shared blame.

He retrieved two cups from a shelf, then poured the honeyed wine she'd gifted him and placed one in front of her.

Ailith looked from the cup to his bare chest, her gaze trailing to the bandaged wound on his shoulder. Where her eyes landed, his skin tingled, alive as if touched.

"Err… I should put on a tunic," he muttered, retreating to grab it from atop the trunk and pulled it over his head. The fabric felt like armor against feelings he hadn't dared acknowledge in years.

"We best eat before it grows cold," he said.

"It's only enough for ye. I already ate." She sipped the wine, avoiding his gaze.

He ignored her words, fetched a second bowl, and carefully served her a small portion before tearing off a chunk of bread to rest on top.

They ate in silence, yet it wasn't uncomfortable. It was… peaceful. As if they'd sat together a thousand times before. Companions forged in something deeper than friendship.

"How's yer wound?" she asked quietly. "Is it healing."

"It is. Barely aches."

She eyed the empty pot. "Would ye like more? I could fetch more."

"No." His voice was gentle but firm. "Ye dinnae need to serve me, Ailith. Ye've done more than enough."

He'd seen her in the past days, carrying bandages to the wounded, pressing cool cloths to burning brows, never stopping, never resting. She moved like a woman with something to prove. Or perhaps something to atone for.

"Where are ye sleeping?"

Ailith gave a small shrug. "Here and there. Teller and I find a corner when we can."

He frowned, and she rushed to add, "It's fine. It's what I want. I feel like… I need to… to make things right."

Without thought, he reached out and took her hand. Her fingers were cold.

"Ailith, ye have mourned. Ye lost yer husband. And now ye've done much to help others. It's time ye rested. Ye've more than paid for anything that ever was."

Her shoulders slumped, and the tears came suddenly, silently, streaking her pale cheeks. "I'm so verra sorry. Please… Please forgive me."

Hendry rose and gently pulled her up into his arms. She was far too light, too fragile, and trembling like a leaf. She buried her face in his chest, clutching at him as though he might keep her from falling.

It was guilt, he realized. She was drowning in it. And much too exhausted.

"I forgive ye, Ailith," he murmured. "Ye are a good woman. A kind soul. Dinnae carry this any longer."

He lifted her and carried her to the bed, laying her down gently and slipping off her shoes and then drew a blanket over her.

"Sleep now. I'll be here to watch over ye."

She blinked up at him, eyes red-rimmed, hopeful but uncertain. "Will ye hold me? Just… until I fall asleep?"

He hesitated only a breath before lying beside her, drawing her into the curve of his body. She nestled into him with a sigh, her cheek against his chest.

He soothed her like he had in another life, when they'd been together, before everything changed, his hand moving slowly down her arm.

"Sleep," he whispered again.

A CARESS STIRRED Ailith from sleep, fingers trailing down her arm. The touch so tender, it brought tears to her eyes. There were too many *if onlys* to count, as her heart filled with hope that she could redeem herself in Hendry's eyes.

He would be the only man she would ever love, and once back in her little cottage in the forest, it was this instance that would help her endure the lonely years to come.

Wishing to feel more of his heat, of his muscular body against hers, she snuggled closer and inhaled the smell of him. Masculine with a scent of what he'd used to bathe in, something herbal. She imagined the rustic cleansing bar moving across the hard planes of his chest, down his flat stomach, and then... She closed her eyes tighter, pushing away thoughts that had the strength to lure her into the depths of passion.

Already her breathing was coming in short gasps, telling him that she no longer slept. However, as his breath continued in a steady rhythm, it was possible he continued to sleep.

Pushing her luck, she stretched upward and pressed a kiss to the juncture of his jaw and neck. The pulsing of his heart steady against her lips.

Hendry instantly reacted, his hold on her tightening, his face turning to hers. "What are ye doing?" There was no recrimination in his expression, merely something akin to curiosity as his gaze moved from hers to her lips. Her throat went dry.

"I-I am sorry. I should nae have…"

When his mouth crashed over hers, Ailith couldn't help the moan that escaped as her as her body flared to life.

Ailith kissed him back with wild abandonment. Clinging to him. Clutching the course fabric of his tunic. Needing. Wanting. Pleading.

When his tongue teased, she gladly accepted the wonderful intrusion. There wasn't a need for talking or any kind of explanation. Their bodies conversed in the language of passion, desire, and raw hunger.

They tore at each other's clothing. Removing the garments clumsily. Yanking away each piece as if it were offensive, not caring where it landed when tossed away.

Not soon enough, skin pressed against skin. Hands roamed over each other's bodies in a dance of reacquaintance.

How beautiful he was. His battle-honed body was strong, thick, and powerful. Ailith wanted to drink him in, but at the moment it was impossible to keep from what both desperately needed.

Once again, they kissed, taking from each other with their mouths, lips, and tongues.

Ailith pulled at him, urging him to cover her with his body and when he came atop her, she almost cried.

Years disappeared and they became the couple who loved each other unconditionally. Their bodies honed to one another. Instinctively knowing what the other wanted and how to bring about the greatest pleasure.

His powerful leg spread hers, and she arched into him the

burning heat so intense, it was almost painful.

Guiding himself, Hendry prodded at her sex, then strong hands slid beneath her and lifted Ailith from the bed as he thrust into her.

It was exactly how she enjoyed lovemaking, not gentle or tentative, not at first. She preferred it hard, fast, and rough.

He was large, thick, and very hard. His manhood delving deep into her, each thrust harder than the last, instinct taking over.

Instead of calming, the fire grew until it consumed her. Ailith thrashed under him, unable to contain her body's reaction as a wave began to crest.

She was mewling by the time she crested, her entire body shuddering, her fingers digging into the bedding as her back arched from the strength of the climax.

Oh, how he knew her. Understood her. Hendry didn't stop. Neither was he gentler. Instead, he continued driving and thrusting harder, his body slick with sweat.

As the second wave grew within, Ailith grabbed Hendry's hips, pulling him deeper. The sounds of their bodies clashing intermingled with his hoarse voice, a melody to her ears.

The tide pulled her under, every inch of her seizing as another release burst. The sounds she made were low and guttural.

Hendry's feral growl filled the space as he arched his back, the tendons of his neck straining from the powerful release.

Drunk with love, Ailith pulled Hendry closer and covered his mouth with hers. The kiss didn't last long as both were pulling in gulps of air.

The weight of his body when it collapsed atop hers was

wonderful. The bedding dipped and allowed her to breathe despite his weight.

Idly, she ran her fingers down his back, glad for his soft grunt of pleasure at her ear. She allowed her hand to slide further down until reaching the roundness of his bottom.

They remained without moving for a long time, still joined, neither wanting to break the bond.

Finally, Hendry slid from her but kept her against him. He pressed kisses to her throat, making a trail down to her shoulder and beyond until taking the tip of her breast into his mouth. Ailith let out a soft hum of enjoyment as his tongue began to swirl around it, flicking and teasing.

So lost was she in the sensations that she gasped when his fingers slid between the folds of her sex.

Hendry caressed her wet, swollen flesh with tenderness, gently circling the sensitive nub. Instantly tingling traveled down her legs and up into her stomach. A flicker of warmth growing into a full-fledged fire with each movement of his fingers.

She reached for him, wrapping her hand around renewed hardness. Automatically his hips moved into the hold. Ailith stroked the silky flesh, loving the way he responded with satisfying moans.

"Stop," Hendry said, pushing her hand away. "I must have ye again. Not in this manner, but fully."

He pulled her over him. "Take me, lass. Take all of me."

Ailith had never made love in this manner, her lovemaking with Brant had been only with him on top.

The mechanics of how it would work seemed obvious, yet she wasn't sure if she was meant to lay upon him or remain upright.

Sensing her confusion, Hendry took her by the hips, lifting her. "Guide me into ye."

She did as he instructed, and he gently lowered her until he filled her in a completely different way. Her eyes rounded; it was as if he'd grown larger, thicker, fuller.

"Remain like this," he gasped out. "Place yer hands upon my chest and lift and lower yer body."

She did as he told her, feeling completely exposed as his hungry eyes took her in. Surprisingly it made her even more aroused.

Lifting and lowering, Ailith soon found the rhythm that suited them, an easy pace, his sex filling her completely.

Soon, although growing weary, she couldn't stop, the nearing release demanding she continue. She wanted to cry with relief when Hendry took her hips, helping her move. She trembled, almost dreading the explosion that was to come. Then she came, her sex milking his as it tightened around him.

Hendry stroked her where they were joined, sending her into an entirely new release, so extreme, her body spasmed.

Through the haze, she was pulled against his chest as Hendry continued moving in and out of her body, once, twice, and then he too lost control.

Ailith collapsed over him, utterly spent. "I love ye so much."

Instantly she regretted blurting out the words and prepared herself to be rejected.

If he was to send her away, she would accept it.

She knew she didn't deserve him.

# CHAPTER FIFTEEN

HIS BODY THRUMMED with life, every nerve tingling in the afterglow of something more than just passion. It was as if he'd been awakened from a long, restless slumber. Though weariness tugged at his limbs, he felt more alive than he had in years. Used. Spent. Cherished. His muscles, sore from effort yet fully sated.

He'd been with others since Ailith, shared laughter and warmth in a lover's bed, but none had left this…this fullness. None had undone him the way she had, with her whispered sighs and the way her lithe body melted over his like warm silk. Ailith had seeped into every breath, every touch. She had given him everything, and for the first time in years, he'd let himself take.

When she'd told him she still loved him, her voice had trembled, the words caught somewhere between hope and fear. She'd braced for rejection. But how could he ever reject the only woman who had ever truly held his heart?

He drew her close, wrapped her in his arms, and pressed a kiss to her hair, breathing in the scent of her, lavender and earth and something uniquely Ailith. He closed his eyes. God above, how could he ever let her go again?

Outside the walls of the cottage, pain still reigned. The wounded and maimed not far from this fragile cocoon of warmth. He could've been one of them. A single misstep, a deeper cut, and his body would've been among those draped on the practice field, never having had this moment. Never feeling her lips on his skin again. Never knowing if ever there he'd ever forgive her.

The heaviness of guilt coiled around his heart. It felt selfish to lie here, wrapped in tenderness, when a world filled with suffering existed just beyond the threshold. But perhaps, just this once, fate had gifted him mercy.

Soon he would rise, don his weapons, and face the reality again. But in this stolen moment, he faced something far more daunting, his own heart. Because here, in this bed, lay the woman who had once broken it.

She'd betrayed him, had not waited for his return. Ailith had believed Brant's lies that he'd been unfaithful. After knowing each other for years, loving each other for years, she'd trusted a near stranger's tales and turned away from him without question.

That she'd then married Brant quickly, perhaps as a salve or as revenge. Whatever the reason, it had been the ultimate strike that had shattered his heart into pieces.

And yet... even as resentment had festered inside him over the years, it had never managed to kill what he felt for her. The ache had dulled, like a wound leaving a scar, yet she held his heart.

He wanted her still. Wanted a life with her. But this time it would be different. He would go with his eyes fully open and not pretend the past hadn't happened.

He would tell her everything, his hurt, his hope, and the raw edges of trust that would need mending. If they were to walk forward together, they'd have to learn one another again. Let love grow slowly, not from the fire of desire alone, but from the embers of honesty and understanding.

And if she was willing to take that journey with him… he would never let her go again.

Ailith moved to lay curled against him, her body warm and still. He felt it then, her quiet trembling, the wet warmth of tears soaking into his chest. Every now and then, she sniffed softly, as though trying to keep the sound of her sorrow hidden.

Hendry's heart clenched at her weeping. Words didn't come, though there was much to say, but he couldn't find a way to begin. He placed his hand at the small of her back, a slow stroke meant to soothe, to speak where words failed.

"I have been angry for so long, Ailith. At ye. At Brant. At myself. Even at God for taking ye from me. The moment everything I cherished vanished, it was as if life no longer mattered."

Ailith listened in silence.

"Aye, I continued in my duties, spent time with my family and even with women." Ailith stiffened and in a selfish way Hendry liked that for a moment she felt what he'd endured when she'd been with another.

He continued, "Through it all, my heart however remained like a heavy stone lodged in my breast. Ye had moved on, stopped loving me."

"I never…"

"Let us not ever pretend that the past didnae happen. Ye must have felt something for Brant. Ye were his wife. Slept next to him for years. I expect that feeling between ye grew."

Ailith nodded. "I did grow to care for him. He was my husband and in some ways kind," she said in a soft voice.

Hendry had to stop from interjecting that lying to her from the start had not been a kind thing to do.

Instead he continued, "I would prefer it if ye and I are completely honest with one another. Even if it is hurtful, I will nae forgive any form of untruth." He let out a breath, bracing, knowing that his words would be raw, but necessary.

"In my heart, I ken ye are the woman for me. That no one will ever make me feel the way ye do. But I cannae say that I love ye."

A sob escaped her lips, sharp and quiet. "I-I understand. W-what can I do?" she stuttered.

Hendry shrugged. "I dinnae ken. I suppose it will take time. What was broken between us will take time to mend. Trust will have to build."

"I hate that we lost so much," she said, fingers curling into the skin of his chest. "That I let someone ruin what we had."

He nodded, his jaw tight. "So do I. But we're here now. I do wish to move forward, I need time to… I dinnae ken… think things through."

"I will wait," she said fiercely, the words trembling with emotion. "I'll wait as long as it takes."

Hendry drew her closer, his arms a vow around her body.

# CHAPTER SIXTEEN

THE GRAY LIGHT of dawn spilled gently through the cottage window, softly illuminating paths across the room, bringing with it a new day.

Ailith lay still, afraid to move, afraid that any shift might wake her and reveal it had all been a dream.

But it wasn't.

His arm was draped protectively around her waist, the warmth of his skin against her back. His chest moving in and out with the steady rhythmic sounds of his breathing.

Hendry asleep with her. It was real.

She blinked, eyes burning as the weight of everything they'd said and what they hadn't, settled over her like another layer of blankets. Her heart ached with it, not from pain, but from the tenderness of a love she had buried long ago, only to find it still alive and stronger than ever.

He stirred behind her, a soft grunt as he came to wakefulness.

"Ye're awake," she whispered, not turning.

"Aye," came his reply, voice gravely with sleep. "I woke earlier but remained still. I didnae wish to disturb ye."

"Ye wouldn't have." She swallowed thickly and rolled onto her back, eyes meeting his. "I've hardly slept. I was afraid if I closed my eyes too long, ye would be gone when I opened them."

His brow furrowed, and he leaned on his elbow to look down at her. "I am nae gone. And I will nae be going far from ye."

Still, her voice trembled. "Ye must go soon from the bed."

He hesitated, then gave a slow nod. "I must. There's still much to do. My men await. I must see about the wounded."

Her chest tightened, and for a moment she hated reality for intruding, for demanding him so soon. But she nodded. "I will help where I can."

Hendry reached out and caught her hand in his, rough fingers cradling hers like they were something precious. "But I swear Ailith, I will return to ye. I wish for a life with ye, not just a moment."

Her throat caught. "And I want one with ye. But… I am uncertain about how we begin again."

He gave her a small, aching smile. "One day at a time. We will take our time, mend what was torn. And if ye will have me, I shall spend every day making ye believe in us again."

Ailith sat up slowly, the blanket falling around her waist. She leaned over and kissed him softly, no passion, just a quiet promise.

"I already do."

Hendry pressed a kiss to her lips and rose from the bed. He added kindling to the fading fire in the hearth, then went about washing up. Obviously, the squire had come inside while they'd slept.

Her cheeks burned at the realization, but she didn't dare take her gaze from him. She enjoyed admiring the nakedness of his body too much.

While he pulled on his breeches, stockings, tunic, and boots, he informed her about his plans for the day. "I will break my fast, then meet with the other leaders and the laird. Then I gather my men and…" His voice broke. "Assign duties to those who remain."

Ailith slid from the bed with the blanket wrapped around her and let Teller, who scratched at the door, out. "How many men did ye lose?"

He let out a long sigh. "Five." Turning away, he walked to get his leather belt from a hook by the hearth and wrapped it around his waist. "I best go."

Moving across the cool floorboards, Ailith went to him and lifted her face to accept a kiss. "I must fetch my donkey and wagon from the stables, then I must go to my cottage. I require clothing; my current set is in a horrible state."

Before she could say more, he took her arm and pulled her against himself. "Someone will have to go with ye. There could still be MacLeods about. Those who could nae escape by sea, and they will be desperate."

"I dinnae wish to take someone away from their duties," Ailith protested. "I will ask the women, I am sure someone can spare clothing."

It was gratifying when he let out a relieved breath. "Once all is settled, I will go with ye. I ken ye will wish to see all is well at yer home."

Ailith wanted to ask more questions, but they'd have time to talk. For now, she would remain in there, spending her days at the keep and nights with Hendry.

DESPITE WASHING UP with the water left in the bucket, she was reluctant to dress. Her clothes were soiled with dried blood and other things she'd rather not think about. She hadn't time to consider much the night before, washing her clothing had been last on her mind.

Crossing to the old trunk at the foot of the bed, she lifted the lid and dug through the neatly folded garments. Most were well-worn and in need of mending, but she found one tunic that, while frayed at the cuffs and thin from years of washing, smelled of cedar and lavender sachets tucked beneath the linens. Clean. That would have to be enough.

She pulled it on over her chemise. It hung a bit loosely, but the fabric was soft and comforting. Her skirts, however, were another matter. With a sigh, she picked up the soiled ones and stepped into them. They crackled faintly with dried blood, and she pushed down the rising unease that threatened to turn her stomach.

Using her fingers to untangle her hair, she braided it. Then laced up her boots, squared her shoulders, and left the cottage.

The moment she stepped out into the morning air, the world met her with stillness, which contrasted starkly after days filled with shouts, hurried footsteps, and the agonized moans of the wounded. The courtyard was damp with dew, the flagstones glistening beneath her feet as she walked across them. Smoke curled lazily from the kitchen chimney, and the scent of ash and fresh bread teased her senses.

Her steps echoed lightly as she crossed the worn stone path, eyes scanning the keep's weathered walls and the distant shapes of stable hands beginning their day. The castle had not yet fully woken, but it breathed with life again. A hum of resilience.

She entered through the kitchen doors, the warmth of the hearth washing over her. The housekeeper greeted her with a brisk nod and tired eyes, quickly informing her that the sick and wounded had been moved into the adjacent chambers to better accommodate care. Ailith sat at the table next to the kitchens, normally used by the servants, and ate a simple meal of bread and porridge.

The great room had changed greatly from the day before. The tables, benches, and floors had been scrubbed. Evergreen sprigs in jugs had been set out to freshen the air and cover the remnant odors of sickness.

There, near the hearth, sat Nala with a large basket of neatly rolled bandages beside her. The young woman looked up, her eyes rimmed with fatigue, but when she saw Ailith, her smile bloomed with quiet relief.

"I am here to help," Ailith said gently, settling into the chair beside her.

Nala exhaled with something close to gratitude. "Ye are a godsend."

Ailith offered a weary smile. "Where are the others?"

"The chambermaids are working the laundry. Ainsley's in with the wounded, helping them break their fast."

Nala's gaze swept over her, lingering on the tunic. Her lips twitched. "I dare nae ask where ye managed to find that."

Ailith laughed softly, the sound surprising herself. "It's Hendry's," she confessed in a whisper, a shy grin tugging at her mouth.

Nala's eyebrows shot up, and then she beamed, eyes sparkling. "I am so very glad to hear it. We were growing tired of the man's constant glum expression."

Ailith's face flushed with warmth. "If I can be forthright... my heart feels lighter as well. It'll be slow going, but...I am hopeful."

Nala leaned in with an impish smile. "Dinnae worry yerself. Alexander himself mentioned how he hoped ye and Hendry would grow closer. Said ye would be good for the man."

The warmth in Ailith's cheeks spread to her chest, a quiet joy taking root.

Of course Nala and her husband confided in one another in bed. She'd nearly forgotten how a couple's bond grew stronger in the hush of night. How soft laughter and whispered truths shared in the dark could weave two souls closer than mere time alone could manage.

For the first time in what felt like years, she allowed herself to hope that she would share moments like those with Hendry.

NALA ROSE FROM her chair and stretched, arms arching overhead as a yawn escaped her. Her dark, soft curls bounced with the motion, catching the light like burnished springs. Ailith watched her for a moment, struck by the woman's beauty. The warm golden hue of her brown skin, the proud line of her jaw, the natural grace she wore like a crown. And yet, Nala carried herself with such ease, such unaffected humility, that ye wondered how she was unaware of the radiance she exuded.

"Come," Nala said with a smile, reaching for Ailith's hand.

"We must find ye something more suitable to wear. This is nae a time for pretty gowns, but we'll no let ye walk about in bloodied skirts."

"I can't go home yet. Not until the roads are safer." Ailith looked down at her stained clothing. "Once I do, I'll wash and return whatever ye lend me. Neatly pressed and free of every speck of dust, I promise."

Nala gave a soft laugh and waved her concern away. "There's no need. The wardrobe is filled with clothes left behind by Alexander's mother. She's gone to live with Gavin and his wife now, on another isle, and the garments are for any woman who finds herself in need."

They left the great room, climbed two flights of stairs, and walked down the corridor. Their steps echoing lightly off the stone walls. Morning sun slanted through high, narrow windows, casting gold light on the stone floor. Inside the chamber, they moved to an old but polished armoire that stood tall near the bed. Nala opened the carved wooden doors with a creak, revealing a trove of carefully arranged garments, folded items, neatly hung skirts, blouses of every shade, and fine woolen vests.

With practiced hands, Nala selected a few pieces and laid them out on the bed: two soft chemises, a pair of earth-toned skirts, three blouses with subtle embroidery at the sleeves, and two warm vests.

"Ye must keep these," Nala said firmly. "Better they warm yer back than be eaten by moths."

She returned to the wardrobe, inspected a few cloaks, and chose a heavy one. "This to keep ye warm." Finally she pulled out a long nightdress of soft cream wool. "And this," she added with a playful grin, "will keep ye warm at night. If necessary," she added with a wink.

Ailith was sure her face flushed scarlet as she let out a groan, hiding her cheeks behind her hands. "I swear, ye are enjoying torturing me."

Nala's laughter bubbled up, light and full of life. "I absolutely am."

The moment lifted something in Ailith, chasing away the heaviness that had followed her since the battle. She hadn't realized how much she'd needed to laugh. For the first time in what felt like days, the air in her lungs felt lighter.

Their laughter must've carried, because a voice called from the doorway.

"What is this wonderful sound I hear?"

They turned to see the laird himself leaning against the doorframe. His dark hair was pulled back into a queue, revealing strong cheekbones and the unmistakable gleam of amusement in his green eyes. He looked every inch the laird, commanding, composed, and yet completely softened as his gaze found his wife.

Something passed between Nala and Alexander in that silent look, something tender and private, a glance that spoke of shared nights and countless whispered promises. A smile tugged at his lips, and Ailith found herself momentarily awed by it.

Then his attention shifted to her.

"How fare ye Ailith?"

She stood quickly, bowing her head. "W-well, my laird. Milady is helping me find garments. Mine… are in need of cleansing."

As soon as the words escaped her mouth, she winced. The laird's gaze swept over her borrowed tunic and filthy skirt. His brows lifted in quiet surprise, but blessedly, he said nothing. Instead, he exchanged a pointed glance with his wife, and Nala had the nerve to smirk.

Heat flared in Ailith's cheeks, then spread down her neck like wildfire.

Alexander recovered swiftly, his tone warm and steady, his expression neutral. "Ye are welcome to remain here as long as ye like. Yer help has not gone unnoticed. I am grateful for all ye have done for my men."

Before Ailith could respond, a familiar sound echoed in the hallway, the rhythmic tap of claws on stone. Teller burst into the room a moment later, tail wagging furiously, yelping in delight. The dog launched himself at Ailith with enough force to nearly knock her backward.

"Oh, Teller!" she laughed, kneeling to gather him in her arms. "I forgot I'd left ye in the courtyard!"

The laird chuckled and crouched down and scratched the dog behind the ears. "Faithful to a fault, these beasts." With one last affectionate pat, he stood, walked over to his wife, and kissed her so thoroughly that Ailith quickly turned away.

When she peeked back, the laird was gone and Nala still looked dazed.

"I will never tire of his kisses," Nala whispered, her voice reverent. She stood frozen for a heartbeat, then blinked herself back to the present. "Come, Teller," she said, pulling herself together. "We'll let yer mistress dress in peace."

Once they were gone, Ailith sat on the edge of the bed. Her fingers brushed over the clothes Nala had left behind, fabrics softer and finer than any she'd worn in years. Perhaps they were not the most luxurious clothes ever stitched, but to her, they were treasures.

Not only for the fabrics, but for what they meant.

A new start on life.

AILITH BALANCED THE stack of freshly rolled bandages in one arm while nudging open the heavy wooden door with her shoulder. The large room had a line of cots along two facing walls, upon which injured men lay. Some slept, while others stared up at the ceiling. The healer was going from man to man, checking how they fared.

The wounded were finally able to rest. Some would heal. Others, she didn't let herself think too long on it.

She stepped in and went to a table against the wall that was being used to hold supplies.

A woman stood next a cot and motioned her forward. "I could use a pair of those."

Ailith brought over the bandages, noting the man in the cot, who's pale face was scrunched from the pain of his injuries.

After depositing half the bandages, she left the room and turned to go to the next one, she nearly collided with a broad chest.

Startled, she gasped and staggered a step back. The bandages wobbled in her arms.

A familiar hand shot out, steadying them, and her.

"I've got ye," Hendry said softly.

For a moment, they simply stared at one another. The air between them thick with all the things they hadn't yet said in the light of day.

He looked every inch the warrior, sword belted at his hip, a faint shadow of exhaustion clinging to the lines around his eyes. But what struck her most was the way his gaze swept over her, slowly, almost reverently.

Her newly acquired blouse hugged her just right, and the vest Nala had insisted she wear cinched at her waist in a way that made her feel pretty. She'd barely thought of it when dressing, but now under Hendry's gaze, she was acutely aware of every thread.

"Ye look…" he began, then cleared his throat, glancing aside for a heartbeat. When he looked back, there was a boyish uncertainty in his eyes that softened her entirely. "Ye look well," he said at last.

Heat flared in her cheeks. "As do ye," she murmured, then instantly regretted it. Saints above, had she just said that?

The corner of his mouth tugged upward, just enough to show he'd noticed her discomfort. "Didn't think we would be this tongue-tied," he admitted, scratching the back of his neck.

"Aye," she said, managing a shy smile. "We went from years of silence to…being, well, acquainted again."

That earned her a soft, surprised chuckle.

A long pause hung between them, filled with a thousand unsaid things, desire, doubt, the fragile thread of something rekindled.

"I will see ye later," Hendry said at last, his voice lower now.

She nodded, eyes lifting to meet his. "Aye, I look forward to it."

Another beat passed. Neither moved.

Then from behind the door, a man gave a pained groan, and they both blinked, startled back into motion.

Hendry took a slow step back, letting her pass.

As she brushed past him, he leaned in just close enough for her to hear: "Ye are beautiful, Ailith."

Her breath caught. She didn't turn, but her fingers clutched the bandages a little tighter, and her lips curved.

## CHAPTER SEVENTEEN

Pain ruled over Liam.

It throbbed through every inch of his body, a merciless, grinding ache that stole his breath and tore raw cries from his throat. His lips were cracked from fever, his mouth dry as sunbaked earth. When another surge of agony twisted through him, his body tensed, a strangled moan escaping before he could stop it. He tried to open his eyes, to drag himself from the thick, muddled haze the herbs kept him in, but the weight of exhaustion anchored him in darkness.

"I'm going to lift yer head now," came a voice, soft, feminine, and impossibly gentle.

Cool fingers slipped beneath his head, and he flinched at the touch, not from pain, but from the shock of something so kind in a world that had become unbearable.

A cup was pressed to his lips, and water trickled into his mouth. The first drop burned down his throat before it soothed, and then he drank greedily, as if that water alone tethered him to the living.

"More," he rasped, the word barely more than a croak.

She lowered his head with careful grace before lifting another cup. He drank until it was gone, then slumped back, eyes fluttering as her voice came again, quieter this time.

"The healer is here. He must inspect yer wounds."

A tremor rolled through him.

"No." The word formed without thought, his body tensing, every muscle screaming in protest. Tears, unbidden and hot, slipped from the corners of his eyes, sliding silently past his temples to soak the linens beneath him.

"I ken," she whispered, sorrow threaded through every syllable. Her hand came to rest on his shoulder, the pressure soothing. "But it must be done."

He didn't want to look, but the healer's familiar voice forced his eyes open, just a sliver. He saw the man's weathered face and the deep lines of exhaustion etched around his mouth.

"I will be as gentle as I can," the healer promised. "Yer leg is crushed and I cannae set it. Had the bones not torn through, I could have bound it days ago and allowed it to set. But it must be cleaned, Liam. If not, rot will take it."

Understanding didn't ease the dread. Knowledge had never dulled pain.

His gaze dropped to the length of his leg, bound tightly in layers of linen from hip to toe. The memory returned with awful clarity, the arrow's sharp sting just before he fell, the thunder of hooves, the horse's wild eyes as it trampled past, already dying, its chest pierced with arrows.

He'd twisted in the last heartbeat of consciousness, rolling just far enough to spare his chest. But the leg… and his arm… hadn't been spared. Bones had shattered like glass.

The sudden exposure of cold air drew him back as the blanket was peeled away.

He shivered violently.

"Cut from here to here," the healer instructed the woman.

"Leave the bandage around his midsection undisturbed. Those wounds are healing well. I'll tend to them tomorrow."

He saw a feminine hand holding a knife.

Liam shut his eyes. Silently praying that darkness would come.

It didn't. He remained lucid. So that when the bandages were cut away and the healer began to work, his hoarse screams filled the chamber, echoing off the stone walls like the wails of a soul being torn from its flesh.

"Liam."

The voice floated through the fog, low and steady, pulling him from the depths of fevered slumber. A warm hand pressed to his forehead, anchoring him further. "Do ye hear me, brother?"

Liam's eyelids felt like stone, but he forced them open. The world was hazy, blurred at the edges, but Hendry's face sharpened into view, drawn tight with concern and something far heavier.

"Ye look worse than I feel," Liam rasped, his voice husky. "Water."

Hendry helped him drink, steady hands cradling his head. The coolness slid down his throat easing the dryness. When the cup was empty, Liam sagged against the pillow, a long breath slipping past his cracked lips.

"Is it midday?" he asked, glancing toward the narrow sliver of light beyond the window.

A faint smile tugged at Hendry's lips. "Late in the day. Ye've been lost to fever for several days."

Liam blinked. "Days?"

Hendry nodded solemnly. "Since the battle, it's been near a fortnight. Ye have been lucid here and there some days. The healer feared ye would nae awaken this time."

Memories surfaced, blurred pain, distant voices, shadows flickering at the edge of consciousness. "How many?" he asked, his voice barely more than a whisper.

He didn't need to explain. Hendry's jaw flexed as if he were biting down on grief.

"Ten and two," he said quietly and began naming them, coming to those Liam called friends and slowly stating the names. "Peter, Lachlan, Colin, and Little Ben."

Liam flinched as if struck. Each name like a knife plummeting into his chest, and he shut his eyes tight to stop the tears. They came anyway, silent and hot, slipping past his lashes into the linen beneath his head.

"Who went to the families?"

"Cynden and Ian," Hendry answered gently. "Yer men would never let the dead go alone. Many rode with them. Even some wounded, those barely able to walk, insisted on paying respects."

Hendry lifted a hand, stopping the question he saw coming. "All of yer men live. Atoll took a blow to the head, but the healer says he'll recover. That he fell may've saved him, they must have mistaken him for dead."

Liam opened his eyes again, finding Hendry's steady gaze. "Will I walk?"

"The healer believes ye will. He does nae ken if ye'll ride again. At least, nae for a time." Hendry's voice cracked then, almost imperceptibly. "But ye're still here, Liam. And that is no small miracle."

Liam stared at the ceiling, the names of his fallen men echoing in his mind. Guilt, grief, and gratitude warred in his chest. He was alive, and they were not.

Long after his friend departed, Liam considered all that had occurred. He'd asked Hendry to tell his men not to come see him. He needed time.

"I BROUGHT BROTH with bits of meat," came the gentle voice. The woman's words tugged Liam from the haze of pain, and he shifted just a bit then stopped when a piercing ache crisscrossed his midsection.

He turned his head, sluggishly, and forgot how to breathe.

There she was.

A lass he'd seen only from a distance in the village, now sitting at his bedside. Her flame-red hair was pinned at her nape, though rebellious curls had escaped, curling around her exquisite face. Blue eyes the color of a cloudless sky met his, and her lips, soft and pink, curved into a smile that made his chest ache in a way that had nothing to do with his wounds.

He'd never spoken to her before, but she'd captured his attention long ago. That hair had turned his head, her curves had held his attention. More than once, he'd found himself searching the crowd at the village square for a glimpse of her. Then he'd seen her once, accompanied by a Ross warrior whose hand gripped her elbow possessively. Liam had turned away. Best not to chase what might already be claimed.

"It is best that ye eat," she said, leaning in, her brow creased with worry. "Ye've nae had a bite in days. The healer asked that I do my best to feed ye all the broth and some bread." She motioned to a small table next to the bed.

Sure his stomach must be caved in by the hollow feel of it, he didn't feel hungry at all. He'd always been a hearty eater, enjoying food as much as he enjoyed admiring women. He scanned her face, glad for the distraction from the pain racking his body.

"Aye, I will eat," he croaked, reaching shakily toward the table.

The lass gave him a smile that reminded him of a mother telling her child they were being naughty. "Nae yet. Let me help ye sit up a bit first."

His body tensed, dread replacing the idea of eating. Moving would hurt. Each time he'd been jostled in order for his bandaging to be changed and his wounds inspected, Liam had ended up drenched in sweat, panting and in so much pain he'd cried out.

He closed his eyes and gave a hesitant nod.

Seeming to understand his reluctance, she gave him a gentle smile. "I will do my best to nae hurt ye."

Her hands were warm, steady, and slow as she slid an arm behind his back and lifted him with surprising strength. "Dinnae help me," she murmured. "I'll stop when ye've had enough."

The floral scent of her hair reminded him of the outdoors, and he inhaled deeply. Her proximity pulled him away from the painful throbbing across his hips.

Once she'd propped him against two rolled blankets, she did something unexpected… She climbed onto the bed, sitting carefully beside him, her hip pressing lightly to his uninjured thigh.

Her cheeks turned a charming shade of pink. "It's easier to

feed ye from this angle."

He wanted to protest, to reclaim his pride, but his limbs trembled from the effort of sitting. Still, he managed a faint smile. "I'm no invalid, lass. I can feed myself."

She gave him a dry look and dipped the spoon into the broth. "Aye, I can see that, ye're shaking like a leaf. I cannae imagine how much pain ye are in." Her expression wasn't one of pity, instead the pinched brow radiated annoyance.

With all the grace of a battlefield surrender, he opened his mouth allowing her to spoon the soup into his mouth.

The broth touched his tongue, warm and savory. He closed his eyes as he swallowed, not just from the pleasure of the food, but from an unidentifiable sensation at how close she was at the moment. Albeit a moment when he wasn't his best, not exactly the picture of masculinity. Yet, Liam had to admit, he enjoyed admiring the beauty.

"What is yer name?" he asked after another sip.

"I'm called Beitris," she said, offering him more soup. "I live in Tokavaig."

Of course he was aware already that she lived somewhere near the village, but her name, he'd not known it. It suited her perfectly.

He studied her as she fed him. Watching the way loose strands of hair framed her delicate features. The way weariness sat at the corners of her mouth and between her brows.

"It's kind of ye, helping the healers," he murmured.

"I came to check on one of the warriors," she said, dipping a piece of bread into the broth. "But once I saw how much work there was to be done, I stayed to help. It felt wrong to do naught."

Of course. A warrior. Probably the same man from the village.

"What's his name?" Liam asked, doing his best to sound casual.

"Keir," she replied, her face brightening. "Ye must ken him. He has served the laird for years."

Keir. Red-haired, muscular build. Liam remembered him now, not one of his own, but known to him. A good enough man.

"Is he still abed?"

"Aye," she said. "Recovering from sword wounds. But healing well."

"He is lucky, then. To have ye looking after him."

Beitris grinned, mischief softening her fatigue. "My brother finds my hovering a curse. Which means, of course, I do it all the more."

He blinked. "Brother?"

She nodded. "Aye. I am younger by a year, but he swears I was born to make his life miserable."

Relief rolled through Liam like a wave lapping the shore's edge. His lips twitched into something close to a smile. "I've a sister myself. Thank the saints she lives far off, or I'd never ken peace."

Too soon, Beitris handed him a cloth to wipe his mouth and gently helped him recline again. He gritted his teeth against the pain but couldn't keep the low groan from escaping.

"I'll be back tomorrow," she said softly, brushing an unruly curl behind her ear before slipping from the room.

Once she'd gone, Liam called for help to relieve himself, a

humbling task. Then he had help shifting positions to avoid sores. Every movement sent fire through his body, and by the time he was settled, he lay panting, damp with sweat. Thankfully, cook brought a hot cider with herbs helped to ease the pain somewhat.

He stared at the rafters above, heart pounding for reasons beyond injury. There was a time not long ago when he would've pursued a lass like Beitris without hesitation. A flirtation. A kiss. Perhaps more.

But now?

He flexed his toes, left foot, then right foot. It hurt, but they moved. That small victory burned with hope and dread. Would he walk unassisted again? Ride? Draw a bow?

Would he ever be a warrior again... or had the battlefield claimed more than just his strength?

Liam closed his eyes and pushed the questions aside, choosing instead to focus on the ache in his muscles as he willed them to move.

For now, pain was better than despair. Pain meant he still lived. And tomorrow, she'd return.

## CHAPTER EIGHTEEN

AILITH CROSSED THE sunlit courtyard, skirts brushing against her ankles, when a familiar streak of black fur barreled toward her. Teller's tongue lolled from the side of his mouth, his amber eyes bright with mischief and contentment. If anything, life at the keep had transformed him. The once scrappy creature now ruled the motley pack of dogs that roamed the grounds, leading them like a furry general teaching the fine arts of chasing shadows, looking pitiful enough to beg scraps, and launching fearless, if usually unsuccessful, hunts for small swift creatures from the nearby woods.

She bent to scratch between his damp ears, wrinkling her nose.

"Ye've been in the mud again. Off to the bath we go," she scolded, though her voice held more fondness than reprimand.

Teller, of course, heard only the promise of adventure. Tail high, he trotted after her toward the edge of the keep where the forest loomed. Just beyond, a narrow creek, its shallow water clear and enticing.

Only when she coaxed the muddy dog into the cold stream, laughing as he paddled in lopsided circles, did Hendry's stern warning echo in her mind: *Never wander alone.*

Her smile faded. She scanned the tree line as the wind

stirred the leaves. The sound made her pulse leap. "Teller, we best go back," she called, the unease sharpening her tone.

The traitorous hound ignored her, darting back to the water's edge and splashing with oblivious glee. "Teller," she hissed, lunging for him. He barked and danced away, paw prints marking the wet earth.

After several failed attempts, she stopped, breathless. "If there was an evildoer nearby, ye've made enough noise to lead him straight to us," she muttered.

"I am leaving," she warned, turning on her heel. Teller, his fur dripping, finally dashed after her, pausing now and then to shake himself, sending icy droplets against her legs. She tried to towel him off with the cloth she'd brought, but each time he slipped away, making a game of it.

She had just straightened from one such failed attempt when she nearly collided with a wall of warm muscle. A startled yelp escaped her as she stumbled back, Teller's bark ringing out at the same moment. Hendry stood before her, hands raised as if to dispel any more fright.

"Oh, Hendry... ye startled me." She avoided his eyes, instead casting a silent glare at Teller, who clearly had failed in his duties as her self-appointed protector.

The dog, momentarily surprised, froze. Then recognition lit his face and with a full-body quiver of delight, Teller launched himself at Hendry as if greeting an old friend after years of absence.

Hendry gave Teller an absent pat on the head, his attention fixed entirely on her. His gaze clung to her face, willing her to meet his eyes.

When she finally did, her breath caught. He was furious.

The sharp set of his jaw, the dark glint in his eyes, the way his lips pressed into a line so tight, all of it radiated restrained anger. He looked past her toward the creek, his voice low and taut.

"I assume ye came alone."

"I... er... aye. With... Teller." The words stumbled out, awkward and thin. "I ken I should have asked Tobin or someone else to come with me." She searched for a plausible excuse, but the effort crumbled. "Surely any wayward MacLeod has been caught by now...or gone."

In the years apart, they'd changed. They'd become different people. She a woman who'd been misled, married someone she didn't love, and then widowed.

He was no longer simply Hendry, but a man who'd been heartbroken by betrayal and tempered in battle. A warrior whose name carried weight in Clan Ross.

They didn't know each other any longer, not really. They were very different people now, very little of who they'd been remained.

So it meant, Ailith had no earthly idea how to soothe his anger, what to say or do to lessen his ire toward her.

"I am truly sorry for worrying ye. I promise it was without thinking that I—"

"Stop," Hendry said, moving closer. "It is because of fear that I am angry. When a stable lad told me ye had gone toward the creek, I imagined so many things."

His statement should have made her feel better, that he acknowledged and explained the reason for his earlier tone was refreshing. Brant would have died before admitting to being wrong about anything. At the same time, Ailith felt worse. Guilty.

"Come," Hendry said, pulling her into his arms. His chest expanding and deflating as he took in a long breath and let it out, his hold on her tightening.

"I dinnae wish to lose ye. Not after waiting so long for this." He pressed a kiss to the top of her head.

Ailith leaned back in his arms, tilting her chin to meet his gaze, and managed a small, apologetic smile. "I truly am sorry. I should nae have come alone. Teller was so muddy, all I could think was that I needed to wash him before letting him into yer cottage."

A shadow flickered across his features, darkening the warmth in his eyes.

"It is yer cottage as well, lass. Do ye nae feel at home here?"

Her breath caught, but she forced herself to shake her head. "I am nae home. My home is the cottage in the forest, Hendry. Nae here at the keep."

The words tasted like a confession she'd been holding too long. For days, she'd rehearsed how she might tell him she intended to return there. She loved their stolen nights, his arms around her, the slow-burning passion that made her forget the years apart. But truth pressed in from every direction.

She was not his wife. And because of that, whispers followed her.

The women of the keep were kind, most of them careful to thank her for tending the wounded, but their eyes told a quieter story. Conversations stilled when she entered a room. She had seen the glances of pity, judgment, perhaps even curiosity. It was no secret she shared his bed, and no blessing of marriage to cloak her in respectability. Widow or no, it was a sin in the eyes of many.

Hendry's fingers slid beneath her chin, guiding her face upward until his gaze anchored hers. Whatever she might have said dissolved as his mouth claimed hers.

The kiss was not gentle. It was more like a flood breaking its banks. Her body surged toward him, answering with a hunger that only he brought out. His touch unraveled the tight knots inside her, loosening the weight she'd carried for years. Every part of him was warmth, strength... life.

It felt like waking after a long winter, the world's colors bleeding back into brilliance.

If he would not marry her, so be it. She would take what she could. His visits. His touch. His voice in the dark. She had lived too long in shadow to turn away from the light he offered, even if it was only borrowed.

Ailith threaded her fingers through Hendry's hair, basking in the feel of his hard body against her, needing him more than words could ever explain.

They broke apart, his darkened eyes delving into hers. "We have time before last meal." He gave her a devilish grin, and she allowed him to lead her back to the cottage.

The door slammed shut behind them and Hendry pushed her against it and lifting her up. She wrapped her legs around his waist, her breathing coming in short pants of anticipation.

"I have nae wanted a woman more than ye," Hendry said. His heated breath against her ear, sending rivulets of desire down her body.

Covering her mouth, his tongue delved in, tangling with hers, and all Ailith knew was that she wanted to take all he would give.

While holding her with one hand, their mouths fused, Hendry fumbled with his breeches until they slid away, and she felt his bare skin between her thighs. He was warm, the fine line of hair that trailed from his chest to below the waist brushed against her sex, fanning the flames of desire.

"Hendry," Ailith gasped out his name. "Please… now."

Guiding himself, Hendry grunted as the blunt end of his manhood teased her entrance. Ailith arched, doing her best to urge him on.

Thankfully, Hendry didn't wait, he thrust his hips forward taking Ailith. Their bodies joined as both let out throaty sounds.

They moved at an unbridled pace, racing to reach a peak from which they could plummet.

Hendry's breathing was harsh, but he didn't slow their pace, as he drove in and out without hesitating, each time taking Ailith higher and closer to being overcome.

She looked down at him, his eyes were closed, lips parted, large body moving in the most sensuous of ways. It was then that her release slammed into her with a surprising force. Ailith cried out, her legs shaking, her sex quaking.

"I am close," Hendry said turning and walking toward the bed with them still joined. He lowered her down, pulled out, and guided her to run. "Get on yer hands and knees," he instructed in a husky breathless voice.

Ailith complied, her body pliant and unsteady.

He pushed her legs further apart, then she felt it, his sex prodding and sliding into her. It was a glorious sensation, and her body instantly responded. She would never tire of him and of the many ways he could drive her to a beautiful madness.

When he took her hips and pushed in, he went deep, still needing more she pushed back. Immediately his response was evident, his member seeming to harden even more as he began moving.

It wasn't long before Ailith was drenched in sweat, her body trembling, her cries muffled by the bedding. What she was saying was irrelevant, each word indistinct and running into the next. She begged for release, she demanded he go harder, then she urged that he not stop.

Hendry growled as he found release, his heated seed spilling into her. Ailith barely noticed as she too was lost to the abyss that claimed her.

"Hendry!" she called out his name, then collapsed onto the bedding, darkness sweeping her away.

When she opened her eyes, she was cradled in Hendry's arms. Ailith smiled up at him, sure she looked a fright, with mussed hair and a splotchy face from the exertion of their lovemaking. And yet, Hendry peered down at her with adoration.

His face was covered in a sheen of perspiration, telling that she'd only been lost for a moment.

"Ye are beautiful. My one and only."

She closed her eyes as his mouth lowered to hers.

This was certainly not the moment to tell him she was to move back to her cottage.

# CHAPTER NINETEEN

THE SKY HUNG low and heavy, a dull sweep of grey that pressed over the training yard like a weight. A fine drizzle slicked the packed earth beneath his boots, beading on his cloak and dripping from the edges in slow, cold rivulets. His men moved in the yard before him, blades flashing in the muted light, the clang of steel against steel ringing through the damp air.

He should have been watching them, correcting a stance, noting a missed opening, but his mind was nowhere near the practice field.

It was back at the cottage.

Back to the moment, only hours ago, when Ailith had stood before him, her words slicing him open.

*I wish to return to my home in the forest.*

He'd felt the ground shift beneath him then, the old wound tearing wide open again. The years of her absence, the cold ache of wanting her and not having her, all of it came roaring back. So he'd done what was easiest. What was safest.

He'd turned his anger into armor.

"As I expected," he'd said, the words cutting sharper than any blade. "Ye'll leave me again."

She'd tried to speak, but he hadn't let her. Wouldn't let her. Instead, he'd walked out. Each step away from her was a wall closing between them. He told himself he was sparing them both the pretense that hearing her reasons would change nothing.

But now... now the drizzle seeped into his bones, and with it came the slow, gnawing truth he should have stayed. Should have listened.

One of the men grunted at a misstep, pulling Hendry's gaze back to the yard. But even as he called out a correction, his chest felt hollow. The sword drills blurred into background noise, a rhythm that no longer matched his own.

"Enough!" he called out signaling the end to the time of practice.

With a muttered curse, he strode from the yard, the damp earth sucking faintly at his boots. The walk to the cottage was longer in the cold, the drizzle sharpening into fine needles of rain against his skin. By the time he reached the small wooden door, he was chilled through, his pulse tight with something he refused to name.

He pushed the door open.

The cottage was still. Too still. The fire in the hearth had burned low, the air cool in a way that told him it hadn't been tended for hours. Her cloak was gone from its peg. The table stood bare, the cup she favored nowhere in sight.

"Ailith?" His voice was rough, the sound of it swallowed by the quiet.

His gaze moved to the rug in front of the hearth, half wishing Teller would be there, head on his paws, sleeping soundly. But it wasn't to be, the rug was empty.

Ailith had gone.

The drizzle outside became a steady rain, the patter against the roof matching the slow, heavy thud of his heart.

For a long moment, Hendry stood in the center of the room, unable to move. The empty space felt wrong, stripped of her warmth, her presence, the quiet sweetness she brought to the air. It was as if the cottage itself had exhaled and gone cold.

HIS CHEST CONSTRICTED with a familiar pang of heartbreak, and for a moment the world tilted. How was he going to survive this again? He closed his eyes, forcing himself to breathe. To think. But all that came was the sound of rain on the roof and the hollow quiet of an empty cottage.

With a sharp turn on his heel, he strode out into the downpour, the cold slapping at his skin like it meant to punish him. His boots pounded over the muddy path toward the keep, each step driven by something between desperation and stubborn pride.

He found Liam in bed, being helped with last meal by one of the healer's helpers. At the sight of Hendry, his friend's brows drew together in mild surprise.

"Ye look like ye've just lost a battle," Liam said, eyeing him warily. "I did nae see Ailith today. Is she awaiting ye in the great room?"

Hendry didn't answer right away. He went to the small hearth, letting the heat lick against his soaked cloak, but it did little to thaw the cold lodged inside him. "She's gone," he said finally, the words tasting bitter.

Liam straightened. "Gone? Gone where?"

"Back to her cottage in the forest. She told me this morning she wished to return to her home."

"Why would she?" Liam's frown deepened, then his tone shifted, cautious. "Does it mean she turned down yer marriage proposal?"

Hendry's head snapped toward him. "What? No. I didnae propose."

The healer's helper snorted but remained silent.

Liam blinked, clearly baffled. "Then why in the name of all that's holy are ye surprised she left?"

Hendry bristled. "She know we are to marry. Of course, as soon as things from the battle settled. It's… it's the natural course."

Liam's brows climbed high, his expression caught between disbelief and pity. "And did ye tell her this? Or did ye expect her to read yer mind like some sorceress?"

The question hit Hendry square in the chest. His mouth opened, but no words came. Images flashed unbidden. He dared a look to the helper, and the woman gave him an annoyed look.

Ailith's guarded eyes that morning. The hesitation in her voice. The way she'd looked at him as if waiting for something he never gave.

A leaden weight settled in his gut. "She didnae ken," he murmured, more to himself than to Liam.

Liam's voice softened, though the edge of reprimand remained. "Hendry… in my experience with women, they prefer to be told what we think and feel. Ye should go after her. But this time, talk to her. Explain everything."

"And propose," the woman added sharply.

Hendry's gaze drifted to the rain-smeared windows, his

heartbeat picking up. He had faced blades, arrows, and the wrath of enemies without flinching. But the thought of laying his heart bare to Ailith felt like the most dangerous battle yet.

# CHAPTER TWENTY

It was a strange, hollow sensation, walking back into her little cottage alone. The moment she stepped inside, the stillness wrapped around her. The air was stale, almost heavy, as if it had been abandoned for much longer than she'd been gone. She pushed the door wider, hoping the light and wind might stir it, but the room remained stubbornly unmoved.

She reached for the broom without thinking, her hands needing something to do. The floor was already clean, yet she swept it anyway. The rhythmic scrape of bristles the only sound. The silence pressed in from every corner, so complete it made her want to crumble to the ground.

Outside, the garden she had once tended with pride was a brittle graveyard of plants. Stems bent and leaves crumbled under her touch. Dry and lifeless. She pulled them up one by one, tossing the withered remains back into the soil. They would serve feeding the soil.

Teller padded after her with uncharacteristic quiet, his tail low, his usual bright energy dimmed. Even when a squirrel darted between two trees, he only lifted his head to watch before settling back at her heels. No bark, no chase.

She patted her loyal companion's head. "Look Teller, did ye see it? A squirrel, there." She pointed to the tree the little creature had scampered up.

It was getting colder, she fed the donkey and placed a blanket over it to keep it warm. Once inside she boiled a pot of beans with scraps of dried meat just as the daylight was fading. She sat before the hearth, staring into the flames without really seeing them.

*Should I have stayed? Waited?*

The questions circled endlessly, wearing grooves into her mind. She'd let her impulsiveness and pride steer her decision, as she had too many times before. And when Hendry, hurt in a way she could hear in the steel of his voice, accused her of leaving him again, she had done the most damning thing of all: she hadn't run after him to explain.

Now, imagining his pain, her chest ached as though she'd been the one struck. Tears slid hot and unbidden down her cheeks. In his eyes, she had abandoned him. Again. And perhaps, in some way, she had.

Teller's soft whimper pulled her from her thoughts. He lay curled before the fire, paws twitching in some dream. Was he chasing something in his sleep? Or simply longing for the warmth of the keep, for the company of the odd little pack they had left behind?

Outside, the wind picked up, slipping through the trees and coaxing the bare branches to scrape against the cottage walls. That sound had once been a comfort to her. A gentle reminder she was not truly alone. Tonight, it was only an echo of how truly alone she was there.

MORNING CAME WITH a stark, biting reminder of her solitude. The chill had seeped into her bones during the night, despite the weight of blankets piled high upon her. At some point, shivering and restless, Ailith had abandoned her bedchamber for the front room. She'd coaxed the fire back to life, then made herself a pallet on the floor beside it, the way she often had in winters past, when the small bedroom became icy cold.

But this night had been different.

Again and again, in the half-world of dreams, she'd reached for Hendry. Her hand would wander across the bedding in search of his warmth, his steady breathing, only to jolt awake at the aching emptiness beside her. Each time, she'd ached for him.

She rolled onto her back now, eyes fixed on the rafters above. How had she once lived years alone without feeling this hollow? And how had only a few days in Hendry's arms unraveled her so completely?

The answer was mercilessly clear, she had been reclaimed. Not just by any man, but by him. Her truest mate. The only one who had ever known her heart and matched its beat so perfectly. The ache in her chest was almost physical, a pull that whispered his name with every breath.

A soft sound drew her gaze to the foot of the blankets, where Teller's head lifted, his dark eyes fixed on her with quiet understanding.

"We are going back," she told him, her voice firm despite the catch in her throat. "We dinnae belong here any longer."

The dog released a long sigh, as though both relieved and weary, before lowering his head again. Soon, a gentle snore was the only reply.

With purpose swelling in her chest, Ailith rose and fed another log to the fire. The crackle and flare of heat was like a promise. She went to her bedchamber, the small space dim and cold, and began to dress. Her hands moved quickly. Adding layers of wool and a heavy cloak before turning to the small chest at the foot of the bed.

She began to pack, each item chosen with care. Her spare gowns folded neatly. The shawl her mother had made for her, soft and worn from years of use. Her hairbrush and comb polished smooth from countless mornings. A handful of ribbons in faded colors, tokens from her sister, which she could never bring herself to discard. She tucked in her sewing kit, a small bundle of linens, and the little carved box that held her most private keepsakes.

The cart would be loaded before midday. And then… to the home where she truly belonged.

Not this life of half-empty rooms and silence.

Home was wherever Hendry was.

This time, she would face him and speak until he understood, until he believed how deeply she loved him. The gossip would still bother her, but whatever discomfort it brought was small in comparison to being away from Hendry.

Her heart belonged with him, and she would not walk away again.

By late morning, the little cart stood ready out in front of the cottage, the donkey stamping its hooves impatiently as if sensing they had somewhere important to be. The air was still sharp with winter's bite, her breath puffing in small clouds as she moved back and forth from cottage to cart.

Teller leapt into the cart without being told, circling once before settling on a folded blanket. His eyes followed her every movement, tail thumping softly against the boards. It was as though he, too, knew this was no simple errand.

Ailith took one last walk through the cottage. Her fingers trailed along the edges of the table, the back of the chair she'd mended herself, the shelf where her few treasured books stood. The fire she'd built that morning had burned down to embers, sending faint curls of smoke up the chimney.

How many nights had she sat here convincing herself she was content? How many mornings had she woken in the cold bedchamber telling herself she didn't need anyone? She had believed it once. But now she knew better. Her heart was no longer in the small cottage that had served as her refuge for so long.

By the door, she paused. Her hand rested on the worn wood, the latch smooth from years of use. For a moment, she almost faltered. Her throat tightening at the thought of leaving it behind. Yet the vision of Hendry's face, of the way he'd looked at her when they'd been together, swept away any lingering doubt.

She stepped outside, pulling the door closed behind her until it latched with a final click. She would not be coming back.

The donkey brayed softly as she climbed onto the seat. She gathered the reins, her heart quickening, not from fear but from the fierce determination thrumming in her veins. Teller shifted, alert now, ears pricked toward the road ahead.

"Let's go. To Hendry. To our new home," she murmured, and the words felt right, true in her mouth.

The cart jolted forward, wheels creaking, and the cottage began to shrink behind her. Ahead lay a winding track through the trees.

THE SUN WAS high as the keep came into view. Ailith pulled the donkey to a stop and climbed down. Teller jumped from the back and raced in circles sniffing the ground in search of new smells.

She stretched while studying the view of the large stone structure. The high walls that surrounded it, and the bridge one had to cross to get passage through its well-guarded gates.

What was Hendry doing at this moment? Sword practice was usually held midday for those not out on patrol duty. He would be standing on the sides, helping with stances and stepping in to show proper defense. In the short time she'd been there, she'd walked out on occasion to watch him work.

Although stern with his men, he was fair when correcting them and often stepped in to ensure they would be well-prepared when having to fight.

A shiver went down her spine, and her stomach tightened just thinking about coming face-to-face with him. There was little doubt in her mind that he remained angry with her.

Standing still and not moving forward was not an option at this point.

"Teller, come!" she called out as she climbed back onto the bench.

BY THE TIME Hendry finally called an end to sword practice, the sun had already dipped low enough to cast long shadows. He'd barely registered half of what the men had done that day; his mind had been firmly fixed on leaving the keep and finding Ailith.

As much as he'd wanted to go and seek Ailith, with so many warriors injured, handing off his duties wasn't an option. The men needed steady guidance, and this wasn't the time for their leader to go sulking off like some lovestruck boy.

Two young warriors, sweat dripping down their temples, trotted up and planted themselves in front of him. They dropped into a stance, clearly expecting pointers. He obliged, correcting their footing, adjusting the angle of the blade. Every minute spent here meant one less chance they'd end up skewered in the next battle, or lopping off their own foot.

Finally, he trudged up the slight incline toward the barrel by the kitchen doors, the promise of cold water calling to him. Dunking a cup into the clear depths, he drank deeply. The relief was short-lived.

A dark blur shot across the courtyard, heading straight for him.

"Teller?" Hendry barely had time to lower the cup before the dog skidded to a halt, tail wagging so hard his whole backside wobbled. The animal let out an excited whine, dancing on his paws.

"What the devil... What are ye doing here? Where's Ailith? Did ye run away?"

The dog pawed his leg and stretched, as if the question was beneath him. Then, catching sight of the other dogs streaking across the yard, Teller took off like an arrow, barking his arrival much to the delight of the other dogs, who all joined in the chorus.

Hendry watched the pack disappear behind the keep, shaking his head. Lucky he had seen Teller, he'd make sure to collect the scoundrel before he set off for Ailith's. She was probably worried and searching for her dog.

He started rehearsing what he'd say to her upon arriving as he crossed the yard. He'd begin by meeting her gaze, steady and sure, and admit he'd been wrong to assume she'd simply stay at the keep without him asking her to marry.

"I wish for ye to be my wife," he began.

He grimaced. "Nae, too formal."

"Ailith, will ye be my wife?"

Still wrong.

"Ailith, will ye marry me?"

Better. But he'd need something before that.

"I dinnae wish for a life without ye. If ye accept being my wife, marrying me, I will be…"

He stopped dead in the path and let out a long, tortured breath. "Ugh. Dunce."

Maybe Liam would ken what to say. His friend was quite adept at spending time with the fairer sex. As for himself, he was apparently more suited for battlefields than courtship.

When he reached his cottage, Tobin was just stepping out, the lad's grin bright enough to make Hendry suspicious.

"Good afternoon, sir. A very good day it is indeed," the squire chirped.

Hendry narrowed his eyes. "Where are ye headed? I require my horse to be saddled. I plan to go, er…leave shortly. First, I'll see Liam."

"I was just going to eat," Tobin said, already edging away.

"Aye, very well. Fill yer belly, then prepare my steed."

The boy gave him a look that landed somewhere between confusion and surprise, never a good sign, but didn't say anything. He turned and trotted toward the stables, where he took his meals with the other stable hands and master.

Hendry watched him go, muttering to himself. "Strange."

THE MOMENT HENDRY stepped into his cottage, he stopped dead.

Something was different.

On the table sat a small cup cradling sprigs of fresh greenery, a simple touch that somehow made the space feel... warmer. A blanket he didn't recognize was draped over the back of a chair, the weave soft and inviting. His gaze moved to the shelves along the far wall, where there were more cups and bowls than he'd owned yesterday. And by the hearth sat a large sewing basket, stuffed full and waiting for use.

He frowned. Why had Tobin brought all this in there?

Then another thought hit him with such force he nearly spun on his heel; he'd walked into the wrong cottage. That must be it. Which would explain the startled look on Tobin's face earlier.

Hurrying back outside, he glanced left, then right. No... this was his cottage. Had someone been given it in his absence? Someone with a wife? Had the laird simply not had time to tell him?

Resolved to gather his belongings and find another place to sleep, he stepped back inside only to freeze in the doorway.

Ailith stepped in from the back door, her arms full of folded clothing. She gasped, eyes going wide.

"Ailith..."

"Hendry..."

They spoke at the same time The words hanging between them like a breath neither dared release.

She recovered first. "I-I have returned. We must talk."

Crossing to the bed, Ailith set the clothes down slowly, as though buying herself a moment before meeting his gaze. Hendry's eyes, however, were already darting around, blanket, dishes, sewing basket, piecing together what it meant. Had she... *moved in?*

Was Liam wrong about Ailith needing to know how he felt? No, Liam was never wrong.

And then she was in front of him, close enough that the faint scent of wildflowers from her hair stirred his senses. She lifted her chin, her lips softening as she searched his face.

"I am so very sorry, Hendry. Please forgive me for leaving so abruptly. I was upset that ye would nae talk to me." Her breath left her in a rush. "I ken ye expected me to break yer heart again, and like a dolt, I did the very worst. I did."

Hendry opened his mouth, but words refused to come. Better to let her speak because obviously he'd lost the ability.

She took his left hand in both of hers, pressing it to her cheek before releasing it. Her skin was warm, her touch steady. "I love ye, Hendry. More than life itself. And if it means living here with ye and ignoring gossips and their snide remarks, so be it."

At that, a flash of anger sparked. His jaw tightened. "Who dared to speak unkindly to ye?"

She shrugged, dismissing it. "It matters not."

It did matter, and he'd address it soon. However, at the moment, it was time for him to speak, to tell her exactly what she meant to him. He glanced up to the rafters, hunting for the right words. "I... I think... We... I mean, ye will want to love and not be married and be a wife..." he paused, groaning.

"The dog is here."

Ailith blinked at him, bewildered. "I am nae sure I understand all of what ye said, but ye should know, I do wish to marry. Though if ye dinnae, then I will accept it. I'd much rather be with ye than alone."

"I do mean to..." His breath stuttered. "What I mean is..." He forced himself to slow, measuring each word. "I wish for nothing more than for ye to be my wife. I planned to come and find ye... to ask ye to marry me."

Her brows drew together. "Are ye sure?"

Cupping his face with her hand, she searched his expression as though to be certain. "I dinnae wish ye to do it because of what I've said. Ye must be sure before asking. Ye've nae even told me for certain how ye feel."

Hendry groaned, a hand scrubbing over his face. "I forgot that part." Then, before she could speak, he met her eyes and let the words come.

"Woman, I love ye so much I ache. I cannae imagine life without ye in it. Ye are more important to me than my allegiance to the laird, aye, more than life itself. I wish to be with ye until the end of my days. I want ye in my bed every night, in my arms, our breaths mingling, our hearts beating together. Marry me, Ailith. I beg of ye. Make this warrior a happy man."

Tears shimmered in her eyes, sliding down her cheeks. Both her hands pressed to her chest, fingers clenched as though holding her heart in place.

"Yes," she whispered, her voice shaking. "Yes. I love ye with all my heart, Hendry. I will be yer wife."

The next moment was a blur. She launched herself into his

arms, and Hendry caught her, holding her tight. Happiness crashed over him so fiercely, he had to blink against the tears burning his own eyes.

For the first time in what felt like a lifetime, he knew, without a single doubt, that his world was exactly as it should be.

# EPILOGUE

*Spring, Ross Keep, Isle of Skye*

AILITH PRESSED THE last mound of soil into place, her fingers curling into the cool earth before brushing it smooth. The tiny shoots she'd planted would soon grow into a garden brimming with vegetables. Food to share not only with Hendry but with the friends and kin who often filled their lives.

Most days, she and Hendry took their meals in the great hall, surrounded by laughter, chatter, and the warmth of the clan. But every so often, they stayed here in their cottage, just the two of them, lingering over a simple supper by the fire. Those nights felt like little pockets of sweetness, quiet and entirely their own.

During the long winter, Hendry and a handful of his men had built an addition to the cottage, transforming it into something far more than she had ever dreamed. A proper bedchamber now opened off the main room, the new hearth cleverly set so its heat warmed both spaces at once. Ailith delighted in showing visitors, especially Ainsley and Nala, how cozy it was when they came to escape the noise of the keep and sit with her, sewing in companionable peace.

The front room had become a comfortable sitting room and kitchen, bright with touches of home. It was a far cry from her small forest cottage. Although she carried fond memories of that place, her heart no longer lived there.

Her old cottage was not abandoned, though. Her sister and brother-in-law had found an elderly couple who'd been cruelly cast out by their kin, and they now called it home. Knowing it sheltered someone again made Ailith glad that it continued to be a home.

Hearing male voices inside, Ailith dusted her apron and smiled. Teller would be along soon, no doubt expecting his dinner, unless, of course, he and his ragtag band of mischief-makers had already charmed the cook into feeding them scraps.

When she stepped inside, her hands flew to her mouth. Hendry was helping Liam ease into a chair, the archer's movements deliberate but determined.

"Ye made it this far!" she said, her smile lighting the room.

"Aye," Liam replied, a trace of a grin on his lips despite the flicker of pain in his eyes. "Further each day. Nae able to ride yet, but I've loosed a few arrows."

Ailith knew, as Hendry had told her, that Liam might never ride again. His left leg and hip had healed stiff, forcing him to drag the leg forward with each step, cane in hand. It was a hard blow for a man who had once moved like the wind and drawn the gaze of every lass in a room.

And yet his spirit had not dimmed. If anything, he fought harder, every day found a way to challenge himself, to adapt, to keep living as a warrior in his own way.

"The laird has asked Liam to take over scribe duties," Hendry told her. "The last scribe's moving to the Isle of Harris to join his wife's clan."

Ailith studied Liam's face. There was no bitterness there, no sadness, only quiet acceptance.

"That is a good thing," she said warmly, squeezing his shoulder. "I have every confidence ye will excel."

She left them to talk and stepped back into the sunlight. As she returned to her garden, her thoughts lingered on Liam's resilience. Warriors trained for battle and for death, but rarely for what could come after injury. She prayed Hendry would see what she saw. That there was always another path, another way to live with honor.

BEITRIS WAS GLAD to have returned to the keep and visit those she'd cared for. Keir had returned for guard duty, and she'd asked to spend the day at the keep. Surprisingly, he'd agreed. Mostly because he knew how much she wished to see the wounded and how they now fared.

The courtyard was busy, chambermaids, kitchen help, and squires crossing with buckets from the well. The sharp ring of steel on steel from the practice yard. But Beitris's gaze found him instantly.

Liam.

He moved with that slow, deliberate stride she'd come to recognize over the past weeks. His cane tapped the ground in a steady rhythm, the stiff drag of his left leg making each step look as though it cost him more effort than he'd ever admit. The spring sun caught on his dark hair, and she saw that he remained a warrior, shoulders broad, gaze fierce, much to handsome for his own good.

Before she could stop herself, she was already calling out. "Liam!"

His head turned toward her, the barest flicker of acknowledgment in his bright blue eyes. She hurried down the steps of the main house, gathering her skirts to keep from stumbling, her boots crunching lightly on the hardened earth. She was glad to see him as he had lingered in her thoughts. The handsome archer was someone she'd never aspire to court her. Especially as his reputation for escorting the prettiest girls in the village to dances and such.

"Let me help ye," she said when she reached him, her fingers light on his forearm.

He went still. His gaze flying to where her hand landed on his arm. Instantly Beitris pulled it back.

"I dinnae need help," he said, his voice cool and clipped.

Her stomach sank. "I only thought…"

"That I could nae walk without ye?" The edge in his tone cut deeper than she'd expected, making heat rise in her cheeks.

"I…" Words faltered on her tongue. She hadn't meant it like that. Hadn't meant to wound the pride she knew he guarded fiercely. "Forgive me. I meant no offence."

His expression softened only a fraction. "Aye. I ken ye meant well." He gave her one last sharp look then he was moving again, his back to her, the steady thump of his cane carrying him farther away.

Beitris stood in the middle of the yard, watching him go, wishing she'd simply kept her hands to herself. Yet even with her embarrassment burning hot, she couldn't ignore the tug in her chest. An ache born not of pity, but of admiration for the stubborn strength in every step he took.

ABOUT AN HOUR after Ailith had gone back to tending her garden, the sound of Hendry's boots on the path pulled her from her thoughts. He knelt beside her, the scent of leather and the warmth of his nearness surrounding her.

"Thank ye," he murmured, pressing a kiss to her temple.

She turned her head with a smile. "For what?"

"For what ye said to Liam. He left here smiling… told me how fortunate it was that we'd found each other again. I think ye helped him more than ye ken."

Her heart swelled. "We are fortunate, are we not?"

"Aye."

Before she could say anything else, he scooped her up from the ground as easily as if she weighed nothing. Dropping her spade, she laughed in surprise as he strode toward the cottage, his grin wicked.

"Allow me to show ye just how happy ye make me," he said, kicking the door closed behind them.

Ailith giggled, wriggling in his hold. "At least let me rinse my hands first!"

TELLER TROTTED UP to the back door, nose lifted to sniff the air. He scratched the door and waited. Muffled sounds came from inside, and he cocked his head, listening. Finally, the dog settled down onto his belly and placed his head on top of his paws. It could be a while before his mistress opened the door. He didn't mind waiting.

In the quiet of that evening, the breeze stirred through the fresh-turned soil, rustling the tender green leaves of Ailith's new garden. Inside, laughter and love filled the walls, wrapping the cottage in a kind of warmth no hearth alone could give. Seasons would come and go, storms would rise and pass, but here, in this place they had built together, everything they planted would grow strong.

## About the Author

*Enticing. Engaging. Romance.*

USA Today Bestselling Author Hildie McQueen writes strong brooding alpha Highlanders who meet their match in feisty brave heroines. If you like stories with a mixture of passion, action, drama and humor, you will love Hildie's storytelling where love wins every single time!

A fan of all things pink, travel, and stationery shops, Hildie resides in eastern Georgia, USA, with her super-hero husband Kurt and two little yappy dogs.

Let's stay in touch, join my NEWSLETTER for free reads, previews of upcoming releases and news about my world!

Printed in Dunstable, United Kingdom

70784437R00109